序　言

英文單字是學習英文的第一步，因為不論你的文法再強，如果不背單字，還是無法將英文朗朗上口。但是要正確地記下單字，卻是一件不容易的事。這時如果有一本好書，能用精緻可愛的插圖來幫助記憶，那該有多好。

「**看圖學英文單字**」就是這樣一本令你愛不釋手的單字手冊。本書一共搜羅了一千四百多個生活常用字彙，每個字彙都配有**插圖**，使你背起單字來，就像看漫畫書一樣地快意輕鬆，在欣賞插圖的同時，不知不覺記住了單字，想忘也忘不了。

本書的每個單字，都與您切身相關，而且天天用得到。舉凡**食衣住行**各類語彙一應俱全，例如各種蔬菜水果及各國美食名稱、男女衣著服飾、居家設備、和海陸空交通工具等等。此外亦包羅從**家庭**（*family*）、**學校**（*school*）到**百貨公司**（*department store*）、**銀行**（*bank*）、**郵局**（*post office*）、**大自然**（*nature*）、**生物**（*life*）等各方面語彙。只要是生活必備的，都可以在這本書中找到。

這種**圖畫式一對一**的單字學習法，也可訓練你不必透過中文來背單字，而採取意像和英文的接收方式，讓讀者直接在腦海中形成單字的印象，這是 think in English 的第一步。久而久之，自然容易養成用英語來思考的習慣。

本書因付梓在即，恐有任何疏漏之處，尚祈各界先進不吝指正為荷。

編者　謹識

CONTENTS

PART 1
人類及家庭生活
Human Beings and Family Life

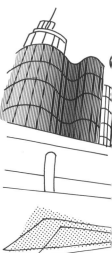

PART 2

社會及文化
Society and Culture

PART 3
生 物
Life

PART 4

宇宙及自然現象
Space and Nature

Part 1

人類及家庭生活

HUMAN BEINGS
AND FAMILY LIFE

❶ 人體　　*Body*

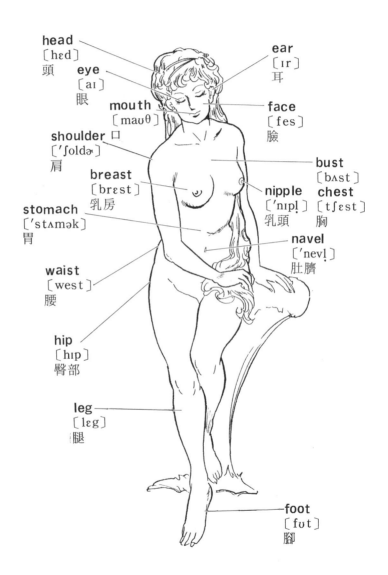

head
〔hɛd〕
頭

eye
〔aɪ〕
眼

mouth
〔maʊθ〕
口

shoulder
〔'ʃoldɚ〕
肩

breast
〔brɛst〕
乳房

stomach
〔'stʌmək〕
胃

waist
〔west〕
腰

hip
〔hɪp〕
臀部

leg
〔lɛg〕
腿

ear
〔ɪr〕
耳

face
〔fes〕
臉

bust
〔bʌst〕

nipple
〔'nɪpḷ〕
乳頭

chest
〔tʃɛst〕
胸

navel
〔'nevḷ〕
肚臍

foot
〔fʊt〕
腳

❷ 臉及口　*Face and Mouth*

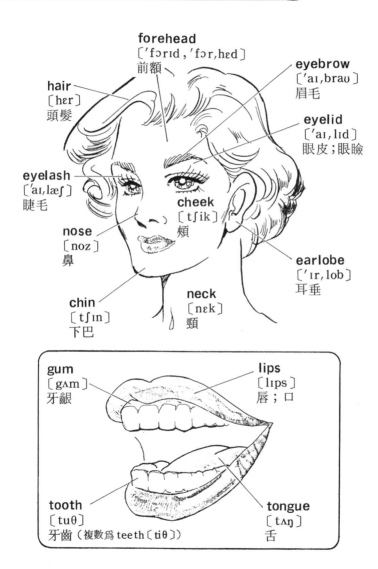

forehead
〔'fɔrɪd,'fɔr,hɛd〕
前額

eyebrow
〔'aɪ,braʊ〕
眉毛

hair
〔hɛr〕
頭髮

eyelid
〔'aɪ,lɪd〕
眼皮；眼瞼

eyelash
〔'aɪ,læʃ〕
睫毛

cheek
〔tʃik〕
頰

nose
〔noz〕
鼻

earlobe
〔'ɪr,lob〕
耳垂

chin
〔tʃɪn〕
下巴

neck
〔nɛk〕
頸

gum
〔gʌm〕
牙齦

lips
〔lɪps〕
唇；口

tooth
〔tuθ〕
牙齒（複數為 teeth〔tiθ〕）

tongue
〔tʌŋ〕
舌

❸ 手及臂 *Hand and Arm*

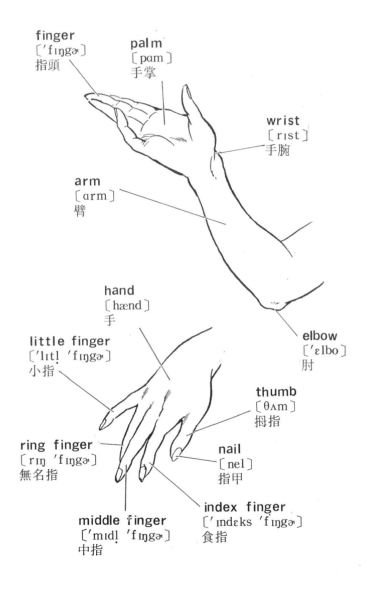

finger
〔'fɪŋgɚ〕
指頭

palm
〔pɑm〕
手掌

wrist
〔rɪst〕
手腕

arm
〔ɑrm〕
臂

hand
〔hænd〕
手

little finger
〔'lɪtl̩ 'fɪŋgɚ〕
小指

elbow
〔'ɛlbo〕
肘

thumb
〔θʌm〕
拇指

ring finger
〔rɪŋ 'fɪŋgɚ〕
無名指

nail
〔nel〕
指甲

middle finger
〔'mɪdl̩ 'fɪŋgɚ〕
中指

index finger
〔'ɪndɛks 'fɪŋgɚ〕
食指

❹ 脚及腿 *Foot and Leg*

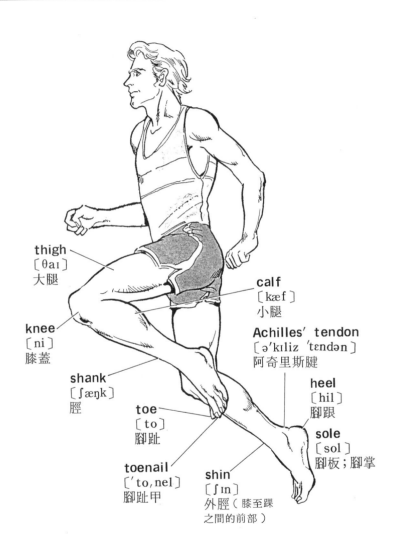

thigh
〔θaɪ〕
大腿

knee
〔ni〕
膝蓋

shank
〔ʃæŋk〕
脛

toe
〔to〕
脚趾

toenail
〔'to,nel〕
脚趾甲

shin
〔ʃɪn〕
外脛（膝至踝
之間的前部）

calf
〔kæf〕
小腿

Achilles' tendon
〔ə'kɪlɪz 'tɛndən〕
阿奇里斯腱

heel
〔hil〕
脚跟

sole
〔sol〕
脚板；脚掌

❺內臟 *Internal Organs*

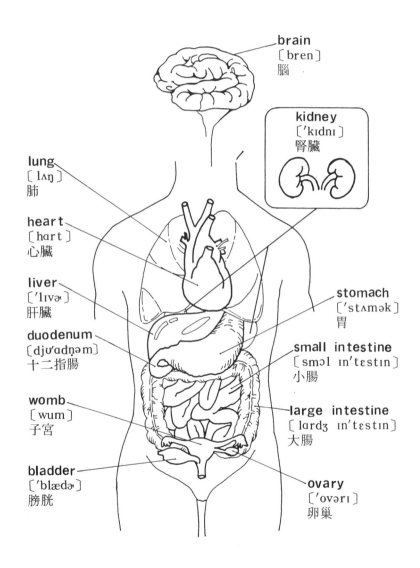

brain
〔bren〕
腦

kidney
〔'kɪdnɪ〕
腎臟

lung
〔lʌŋ〕
肺

heart
〔hɑrt〕
心臟

liver
〔'lɪvɚ〕
肝臟

duodenum
〔djʊ'ɑdŋəm〕
十二指腸

womb
〔wum〕
子宮

bladder
〔'blædɚ〕
膀胱

stomach
〔'stʌmək〕
胃

small intestine
〔smɔl ɪn'tɛstɪn〕
小腸

large intestine
〔lɑrdʒ ɪn'tɛstɪn〕
大腸

ovary
〔'ovərɪ〕
卵巢

❻骨骼及肌肉　*Skeleton and Muscle*

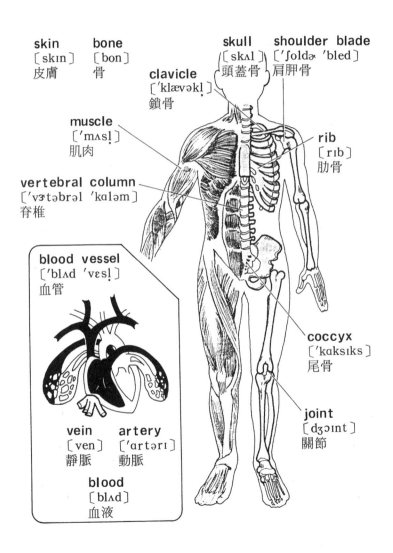

skin
〔skɪn〕
皮膚

bone
〔bon〕
骨

skull
〔skʌl〕
頭蓋骨

shoulder blade
〔'ʃoldɚ 'bled〕
肩胛骨

clavicle
〔'klævəkl〕
鎖骨

muscle
〔'mʌsl̩〕
肌肉

rib
〔rɪb〕
肋骨

vertebral column
〔'vɝtəbrəl 'kɑləm〕
脊椎

blood vessel
〔'blʌd 'vɛsl̩〕
血管

vein
〔ven〕
靜脈

artery
〔'ɑrtərɪ〕
動脈

blood
〔blʌd〕
血液

coccyx
〔'kɑksɪks〕
尾骨

joint
〔dʒɔɪnt〕
關節

❼家庭　*Family*

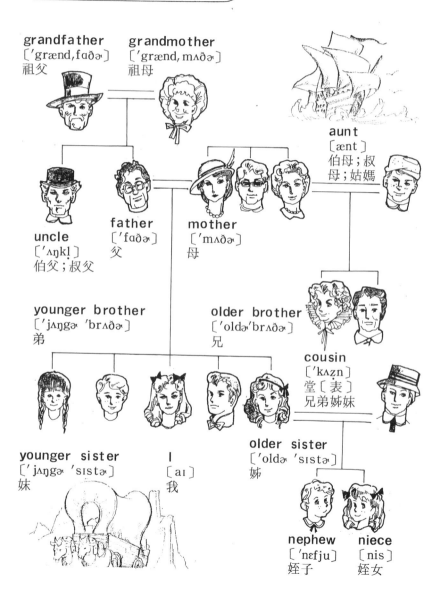

grandfather
〔'grænd,faðɚ〕
祖父

grandmother
〔'grænd,mʌðɚ〕
祖母

aunt
〔ænt〕
伯母;叔母;姑媽

uncle
〔'ʌŋkl〕
伯父;叔父

father
〔'faðɚ〕
父

mother
〔'mʌðɚ〕
母

younger brother
〔'jʌŋgɚ 'brʌðɚ〕
弟

older brother
〔'oldɚ'brʌðɚ〕
兄

cousin
〔'kʌzn〕
堂〔表〕
兄弟姊妹

younger sister
〔'jʌŋgɚ 'sɪstɚ〕
妹

I
〔aɪ〕
我

older sister
〔'oldɚ 'sɪstɚ〕
姊

nephew
〔'nɛfju〕
姪子

niece
〔nis〕
姪女

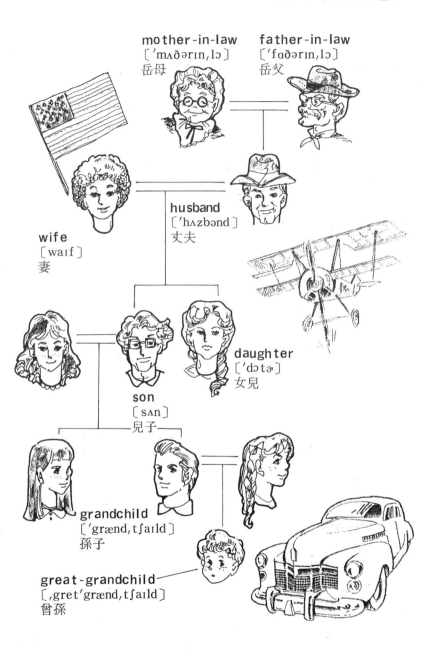

mother-in-law
〔'mʌðərɪn,lɔ〕
岳母

father-in-law
〔'fɑðərɪn,lɔ〕
岳父

husband
〔'hʌzbənd〕
丈夫

wife
〔waɪf〕
妻

daughter
〔'dɔtɚ〕
女兒

son
〔sʌn〕
兒子

grandchild
〔'grænd,tʃaɪld〕
孫子

great-grandchild
〔,gret'grænd,tʃaɪld〕
曾孫

❽人的一生　*Human Life*

school days
〔'skul ˌdez〕
學生時代

childhood
〔'tʃaɪld,hʊd〕
兒童時期

babyhood
〔'bebɪ,hʊd〕
嬰兒時代

entrance
〔'ɛntrəns〕
入學

graduation
〔ˌgrædʒʊ'eʃən〕
畢業

birth
〔bɝθ〕
誕生

teen-ager
〔'tin,edʒɚ〕
十幾歲的少年（少女）

single/unmarried
〔'sɪŋgl〕/〔ʌn'mærɪd〕
獨身

bachelor
〔'bætʃələ〕
單身漢

youth
〔juθ〕
青年期

getting a job
〔'gɛtɪŋ ə dʒɑb〕
就職

unmarried woman
〔ʌn'mærɪd 'wʊmən〕
單身女子

old age
〔'old ˌedʒ〕
老年

middle age
〔'mɪdl ˌedʒ〕
中年期；壯年期

adulthood
〔ə'dʌlthʊd〕
成年期

adult
〔ə'dʌlt〕
成人

retirement
〔rɪ'taɪrmənt〕
退休

death
〔dɛθ〕
死

widow
〔'wɪdo〕
寡婦

widower
〔'wɪdəwɚ〕
鰥夫

grave
〔grev〕
墳墓

funeral
〔'fjunərəl〕
葬禮

divorce
〔də'vɔrs〕
離婚

wedding
〔'wɛdɪŋ〕
結婚典禮

engagement
〔ɪn'gedʒmənt〕
訂婚；婚約

marriage
〔'mærɪdʒ〕
結婚

❾ 男裝　　*Men's Clothes*

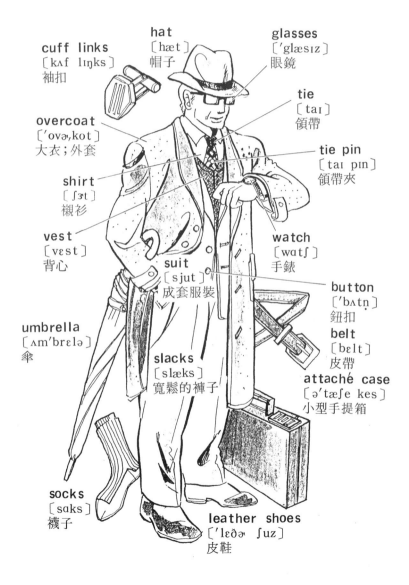

cuff links
〔kʌf lɪŋks〕
袖扣

hat
〔hæt〕
帽子

glasses
〔'glæsɪz〕
眼鏡

tie
〔taɪ〕
領帶

tie pin
〔taɪ pɪn〕
領帶夾

overcoat
〔'ovɚ,kot〕
大衣；外套

shirt
〔ʃɝt〕
襯衫

vest
〔vɛst〕
背心

watch
〔watʃ〕
手錶

suit
〔sjut〕
成套服裝

button
〔'bʌtn̩〕
鈕扣

belt
〔bɛlt〕
皮帶

umbrella
〔ʌm'brɛlə〕
傘

slacks
〔slæks〕
寬鬆的褲子

attaché case
〔ə'tæʃe kes〕
小型手提箱

socks
〔saks〕
襪子

leather shoes
〔'lɛðɚ ʃuz〕
皮鞋

⑩女裝　*Women's Clothes*

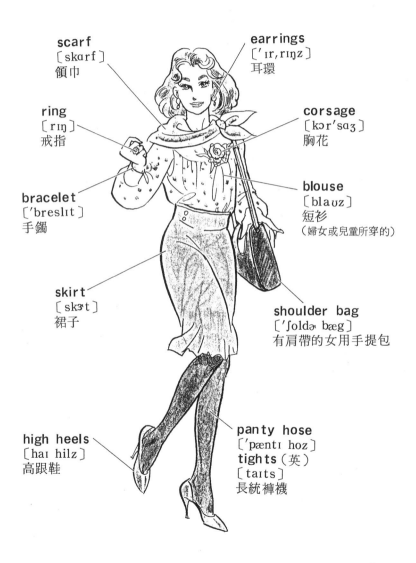

scarf
〔skɑrf〕
領巾

ring
〔rɪŋ〕
戒指

bracelet
〔'breslɪt〕
手鐲

skirt
〔skɝt〕
裙子

high heels
〔haɪ hilz〕
高跟鞋

earrings
〔'ɪr,rɪŋz〕
耳環

corsage
〔kɔr'sɑʒ〕
胸花

blouse
〔blaʊz〕
短衫
（婦女或兒童所穿的）

shoulder bag
〔'ʃoldɚ bæg〕
有肩帶的女用手提包

panty hose
〔'pæntɪ hoz〕
tights（英）
〔taɪts〕
長統褲襪

⑪ 內衣褲　*Underwear*

underpants
〔ˈʌndəˌpænts〕
內褲

undershirt
〔ˈʌndəˌʃɝt〕
vest（英）
〔vɛst〕
汗衫；貼身內衣

corset
〔ˈkɔrsɪt〕
女用束腹

slip
〔ˈslɪp〕
套裙

briefs
〔brifs〕
貼身短內褲

chemise
〔ʃəˈmiz〕
襯裙
（英國維多利亞時代末期
女用似襯衫的內衣）

garter
〔ˈɡɑrtə〕
襪帶

scanties
〔ˈskæntɪz〕
bikini underpants（英）
〔bɪˈkɪnɪ ˈʌndəˌpænts〕
三角褲

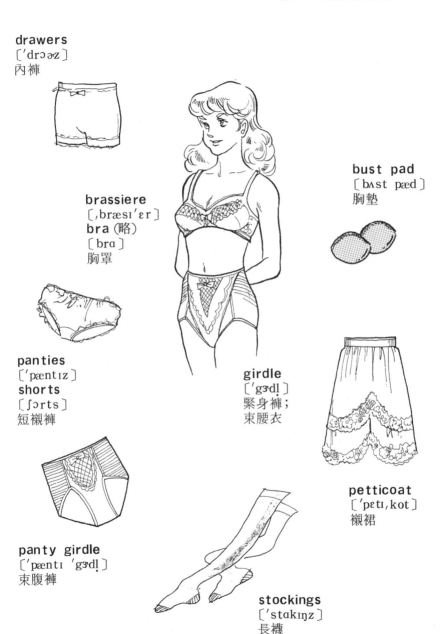

drawers
〔'drɔəz〕
內褲

brassiere
〔,bræsɪ'ɛr〕
bra (略)
〔brɑ〕
胸罩

bust pad
〔bʌst pæd〕
胸墊

panties
〔'pæntɪz〕
shorts
〔ʃɔrts〕
短襯褲

girdle
〔'gɝdl〕
緊身褲；
束腰衣

panty girdle
〔'pæntɪ 'gɝdl〕
束腹褲

petticoat
〔'pɛtɪ,kot〕
襯裙

stockings
〔'stɑkɪŋz〕
長襪

⑫ 正式的服裝　*Formal Dress*

evening attire
〔'ivnɪŋ ə'taɪr〕
晚禮服

swallow-tailed coat
〔'swɑlo,teld kot〕
燕尾服

cocktail dress
〔'kɑk,tel drɛs〕
鷄尾酒會穿的半正式女裝

evening dress
〔'ivnɪŋ drɛs〕
晚禮服

morning coat
〔'mɔrnɪŋ kot〕
大禮服（男士的）

fur coat
〔fɝ kot〕
皮大衣

dress
〔drɛs〕
洋裝

tuxedo
〔tʌk'sido〕
dinner jacket（英）
〔'dɪnɚ 'dʒækɪt〕
男人穿的無尾
半正式晚禮服

⑬ 非正式的服裝　*Informal Dress*

jumper
〔'dʒʌmpɚ〕
短外衣

Safari coat
〔sə'fɑrı kot〕
狩獵裝

windbreaker
〔'wınd,brekɚ〕
皮製防風夾克
（腰部及袖口有鬆緊
帶，運動時所穿著）

duffle coat
〔'dʌfl kot〕
連風帽之粗呢大衣

polo shirt
〔'polo ʃɝt〕
套頭棉衫

trench coat
〔trɛntʃ kot〕
（有帶的）軍用
防水雨衣

jeans jacket
〔dʒinz 'dʒækıt〕
牛仔衣（斜紋布夾克）

blazer
〔'blezɚ〕
顏色鮮明的
寬鬆外衣
（常以絨布製成，用
於運動，其顏色常
代表某一團體）

sweater
〔'swɛtɚ〕
毛衣

jeans
〔dʒinz〕
牛仔褲
（斜紋布製
的工作褲）

slacks
〔slæks〕
寬鬆長褲

pantaloons
〔,pæntl'unz〕
褲子

cardigan
〔'kɑrdıgən〕
羊毛夾克

tight skirt
〔taɪt skɝt〕
窄裙

miniskirt
〔'mɪnɪ,skɝt〕
迷你裙

Bermuda shorts
〔bəˈmjudə ʃɔrts〕
百慕達式短褲（長達膝上
一至兩英寸，成年男女的便裝）

shorts
〔ʃɔrts〕
短褲

cape
〔kep〕
披肩

topper
〔'tɑpɚ〕
女寬鬆外衣

mantle
〔'mæntl〕
斗篷；無
袖外套

anorak
〔'ɑnə,rɑk〕
有兜帽的夾克

down jacket
〔daʊn 'dʒækɪt〕
軟毛夾克

culottes
〔kjʊˈlɑts〕
裙褲

pants
〔pænts〕
trousers (英)
〔'traʊzɚz〕
長褲

parka
〔'pɑrkə〕
附頭巾之
長羊毛衫

⑭配件 *Accessories*

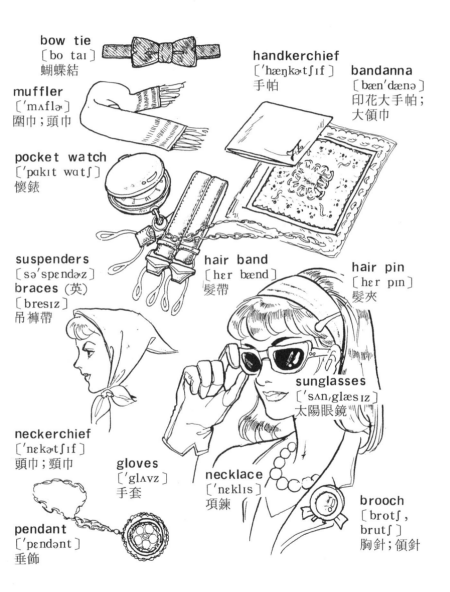

bow tie
〔bo taɪ〕
蝴蝶結

muffler
〔ˈmʌflə〕
圍巾；頭巾

handkerchief
〔ˈhæŋkətʃɪf〕
手帕

bandanna
〔bænˈdænə〕
印花大手帕；
大領巾

pocket watch
〔ˈpɑkɪt wɑtʃ〕
懷錶

suspenders
〔səˈspendəz〕
braces(英)
〔bresɪz〕
吊褲帶

hair band
〔hɛr bænd〕
髮帶

hair pin
〔hɛr pɪn〕
髮夾

sunglasses
〔ˈsʌnˌglæsɪz〕
太陽眼鏡

neckerchief
〔ˈnɛkətʃɪf〕
頭巾；頸巾

gloves
〔ˈglʌvz〕
手套

necklace
〔ˈnɛklɪs〕
項鍊

brooch
〔brotʃ,
brutʃ〕
胸針；領針

pendant
〔ˈpɛndənt〕
垂飾

⑮鞋及帽子 *Shoes and Hats*

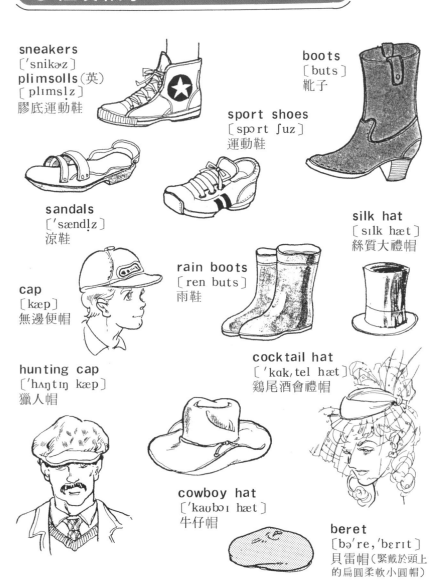

sneakers
〔'snikəz〕
plimsolls(英)
〔'plɪmslz〕
膠底運動鞋

boots
〔buts〕
靴子

sport shoes
〔spɔrt ʃuz〕
運動鞋

sandals
〔'sændlz〕
涼鞋

silk hat
〔sɪlk hæt〕
絲質大禮帽

cap
〔kæp〕
無邊便帽

rain boots
〔ren buts〕
雨鞋

hunting cap
〔'hʌntɪŋ kæp〕
獵人帽

cocktail hat
〔'kɑk,tel hæt〕
鷄尾酒會禮帽

cowboy hat
〔'kaʊbɔɪ hæt〕
牛仔帽

beret
〔bə're, 'bɛrɪt〕
貝雷帽(緊戴於頭上
的扁圓柔軟小圓帽)

⑯袋子類　*Bags*

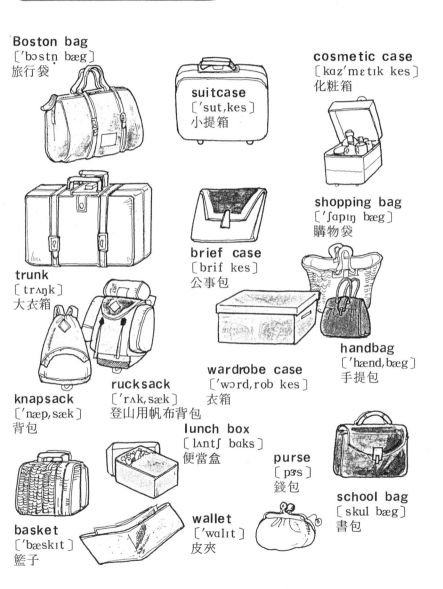

Boston bag
〔'bɔstn̩ bæg〕
旅行袋

suitcase
〔'sut,kes〕
小提箱

cosmetic case
〔kɑz'mɛtɪk kes〕
化粧箱

trunk
〔trʌŋk〕
大衣箱

brief case
〔brif kes〕
公事包

shopping bag
〔'ʃɑpɪŋ bæg〕
購物袋

knapsack
〔'næp,sæk〕
背包

rucksack
〔'rʌk,sæk〕
登山用帆布背包

wardrobe case
〔'wɔrd,rob kes〕
衣箱

handbag
〔'hænd,bæg〕
手提包

lunch box
〔lʌntʃ bɑks〕
便當盒

purse
〔pɝs〕
錢包

school bag
〔skul bæg〕
書包

basket
〔'bæskɪt〕
籃子

wallet
〔'wɑlɪt〕
皮夾

⓱ 肉類　　*Meat*

pork
〔pɔrk〕
豬肉

beef
〔bif〕
牛肉

veal
〔vil〕
小牛肉

mutton
〔'mʌtn̩〕
羊肉

chicken
〔'tʃɪkɪn〕
鷄肉

lamb
〔læm〕
羔羊肉

turkey
〔'tɝkɪ〕
火鷄

roast
〔rost〕
烤肉

tongue
〔tʌŋ〕
（牛、羊等的）
舌肉

liver
〔'lɪvɚ〕
肝

bacon
〔'bekən〕
醃薰豬肉

ham
〔hæm〕
火腿

sausage
〔'sɔsɪdʒ〕
臘腸；香腸

wiener
〔'winɚ〕
燻香腸

corned beef
〔kɔrnd bif〕
醃牛肉

salami
〔sə'lɑmɪ〕
義大利臘腸

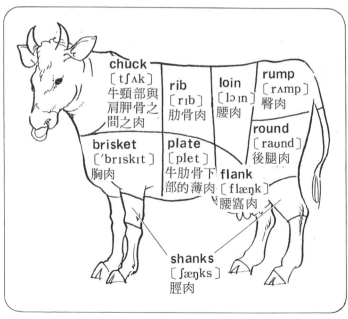

chuck
〔tʃʌk〕
牛頸部與
肩胛骨之
間之肉

rib
〔rɪb〕
肋骨肉

loin
〔lɔɪn〕
腰肉

rump
〔rʌmp〕
臀肉

round
〔raund〕
後腿肉

brisket
〔'brɪskɪt〕
胸肉

plate
〔plet〕
牛肋骨下
部的薄肉

flank
〔flæŋk〕
腰窩肉

shanks
〔ʃæŋks〕
脛肉

⑱蔬菜 *Vegetables*

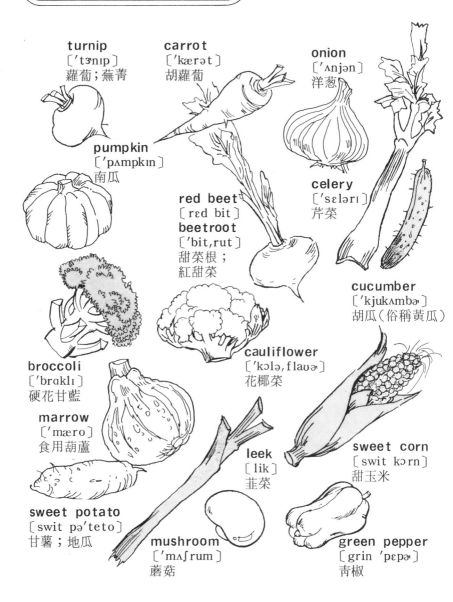

turnip
〔ˈtɝnɪp〕
蘿蔔;蕪菁

carrot
〔ˈkærət〕
胡蘿蔔

onion
〔ˈʌnjən〕
洋葱

pumpkin
〔ˈpʌmpkɪn〕
南瓜

celery
〔ˈsɛlərɪ〕
芹菜

red beet
〔rɛd bit〕
beetroot
〔ˈbit,rut〕
甜菜根;
紅甜菜

cucumber
〔ˈkjukʌmbɚ〕
胡瓜(俗稱黃瓜)

broccoli
〔ˈbrɑklɪ〕
硬花甘藍

cauliflower
〔ˈkɔlə,flauɚ〕
花椰菜

marrow
〔ˈmæro〕
食用葫蘆

leek
〔lik〕
韮菜

sweet corn
〔swit kɔrn〕
甜玉米

sweet potato
〔swit pəˈteto〕
甘薯;地瓜

mushroom
〔ˈmʌʃrum〕
蘑菇

green pepper
〔grin ˈpɛpɚ〕
青椒

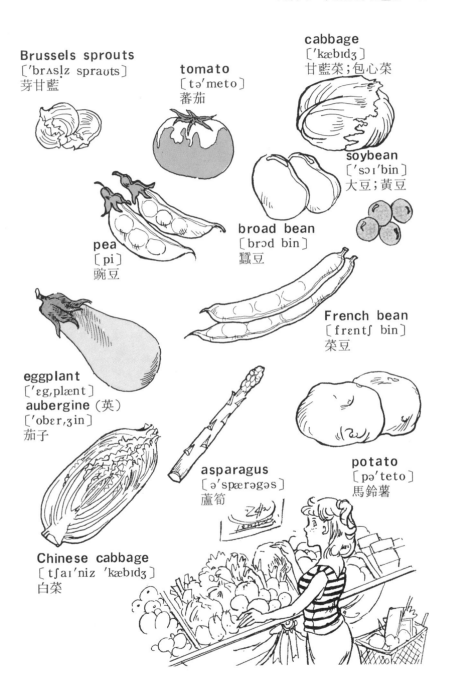

Brussels sprouts
〔'brʌslz spraʊts〕
芽甘藍

tomato
〔tə'meto〕
蕃茄

cabbage
〔'kæbɪdʒ〕
甘藍菜；包心菜

soybean
〔'sɔɪ'bin〕
大豆；黃豆

pea
〔pi〕
豌豆

broad bean
〔brɔd bin〕
蠶豆

French bean
〔frɛntʃ bin〕
菜豆

eggplant
〔'ɛg,plænt〕
aubergine (英)
〔'obɛr,ʒin〕
茄子

asparagus
〔ə'spærəgəs〕
蘆筍

potato
〔pə'teto〕
馬鈴薯

Chinese cabbage
〔tʃaɪ'niz 'kæbɪdʒ〕
白菜

ⓙ 水果　　　*Fruits*

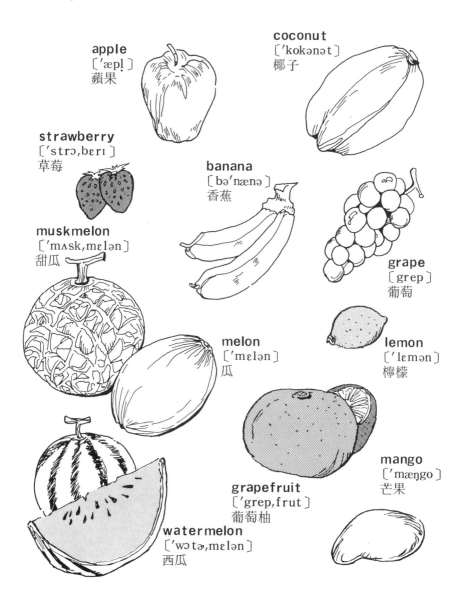

apple
〔'æp!〕
蘋果

coconut
〔'kokənət〕
椰子

strawberry
〔'strɔ,bɛrɪ〕
草莓

banana
〔bə'nænə〕
香蕉

grape
〔grep〕
葡萄

muskmelon
〔'mʌsk,mɛlən〕
甜瓜

melon
〔'mɛlən〕
瓜

lemon
〔'lɛmən〕
檸檬

mango
〔'mæŋgo〕
芒果

grapefruit
〔'grep,frut〕
葡萄柚

watermelon
〔'wɔtɚ,mɛlən〕
西瓜

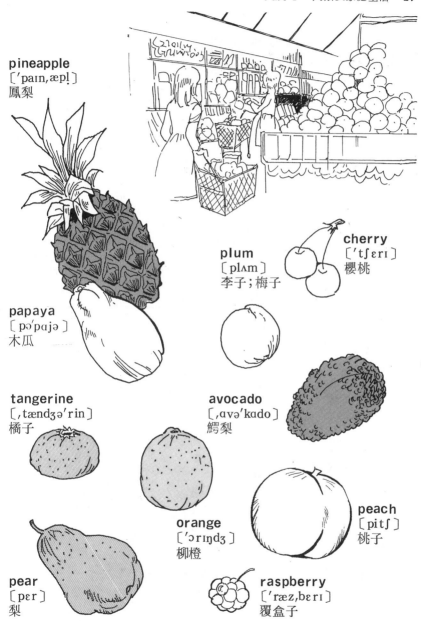

pineapple
〔'paɪn,æpḷ〕
鳳梨

papaya
〔pə'pɑjə〕
木瓜

plum
〔plʌm〕
李子;梅子

cherry
〔'tʃɛrɪ〕
櫻桃

tangerine
〔,tændʒə'rin〕
橘子

avocado
〔,ɑvə'kɑdo〕
鱷梨

orange
〔'ɔrɪndʒ〕
柳橙

peach
〔pitʃ〕
桃子

pear
〔pɛr〕
梨

raspberry
〔'ræz,bɛrɪ〕
覆盒子

⓴菜餚   *Dishes*

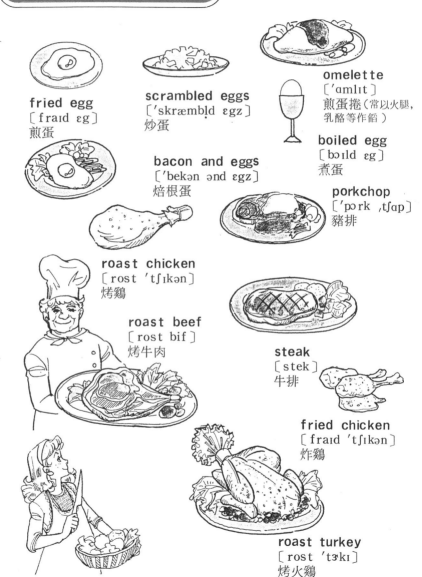

fried egg
〔fraɪd ɛg〕
煎蛋

scrambled eggs
〔'skræmbḷd ɛgz〕
炒蛋

bacon and eggs
〔'bekən ənd ɛgz〕
焙根蛋

omelette
〔'ɑmlɪt〕
煎蛋捲（常以火腿，
乳酪等作餡）

boiled egg
〔bɔɪld ɛg〕
煮蛋

porkchop
〔'pɔrk ˌtʃɑp〕
豬排

roast chicken
〔rost 'tʃɪkən〕
烤鷄

roast beef
〔rost bif〕
烤牛肉

steak
〔stek〕
牛排

fried chicken
〔fraɪd 'tʃɪkən〕
炸鷄

roast turkey
〔rost 'tɝkɪ〕
烤火鷄

potage／thick soup
〔po'taʒ〕／〔θɪk sup〕
濃湯

consommé／clear soup
〔,kɑnsə'me〕／〔klɪr sup〕
清湯

beef stew
〔bif stju〕
燉牛肉

seafood salad
〔'si,fud 'sæləd〕
海鮮沙拉

green salad
〔grin 'sæləd〕
蔬菜沙拉

french fries
〔frɛntʃ fraɪz〕
chips（英）
〔tʃɪps〕
炸薯條

pizza
〔'pitsə〕
比薩餅

hamburger
〔'hæmbɜgɚ〕
漢堡

spaghetti
〔spə'gɛtɪ〕
義大利麵

sandwich
〔'sændwɪtʃ〕
三明治

apple pie
〔'æpl paɪ〕
蘋果派

bread
〔brɛd〕
麵包

toast
〔tost〕
土司

pumpkin pie
〔'pʌmpkɪn paɪ〕
南瓜派

doughnut
〔'donət〕
甜甜圈

cake
〔kek〕
蛋糕

hot dog
〔hɑt dɔg〕
熱狗

yoghurt
〔'jogɚt〕
優格（酸乳酪）

㉑ 調味料 *Seasoning*

salad oil
〔'sæləd ɔɪl〕
沙拉油

bread crumbs
〔brɛd krʌmz〕
麵包屑

baking powder
〔'bekɪŋ 'paʊdɚ〕
醱粉

dressing
〔'drɛsɪŋ〕
調味汁

flour
〔flaʊr〕
麵粉

spices
〔spaɪsɪz〕
香料

salt
〔sɔlt〕
鹽

pepper
〔'pɛpɚ〕
胡椒

seasonings
〔'siznɪŋz〕
調味料

ketchup
〔'kɛtʃəp〕
蕃茄醬

soy sauce
〔sɔɪ sɔs〕
醬油

sugar
〔'ʃʊgɚ〕
糖

chili sauce
〔'tʃɪlɪ sɔs〕
咖哩醬

vinegar
〔'vɪnɪgɚ〕
醋

㉒點心　*Snacks*

potato chips/crisps（英）
〔pəˈteto tʃɪps〕/〔krɪsps〕
炸馬鈴薯片

cookie/biscuit（英）
〔ˈkʊkɪ〕/〔ˈbɪskɪt〕
餅乾

candy
〔ˈkændɪ〕
糖果

chocolate
〔ˈtʃɑkəlɪt〕
巧克力

ice cream
〔aɪs krim〕
冰淇淋

pudding
〔ˈpʊdɪŋ〕

cream caramel（英）
〔krim ˈkærəml〕
布丁

biscuit
〔ˈbɪskɪt〕
小甜麵包

chewing gum
〔ˈtʃʊɪŋ gʌm〕
口香糖

popcorn
〔ˈpɑp,kɔrn〕
爆米花

cracker
〔ˈkrækə〕
薄脆的餅乾

jelly
〔ˈdʒɛlɪ〕
果凍

㉓飲料及酒　　*Drinks and Liquors*

milk
〔mɪlk〕
牛奶

pop
〔pɑp〕
fizz（英）
〔fɪz〕
汽水

Coke
〔kok〕
可樂

juice
〔dʒus〕
果汁

coffee
〔ˈkɔfɪ〕
咖啡

tea
〔ti〕
茶

cocoa
〔ˈkoko〕
可可

beer
〔bɪr〕
啤酒

Scotch
〔skɑtʃ〕
蘇格蘭威
士忌酒

whiskey
〔'hwɪskɪ〕
威士忌酒

bourbon
〔'bʊrbən〕
波旁威士忌
酒（以玉蜀黍
釀成）

brandy
〔'brændɪ〕
白蘭地

gin
〔dʒɪn〕
琴酒

cocktail
〔'kɑk,tel〕
雞尾酒

wine
〔waɪn〕
葡萄酒
水果酒

sake
〔'sɑkɪ〕
日本清酒

champagne
〔ʃæm'pen〕
香檳酒

㉔房子外觀 *House Exterior*

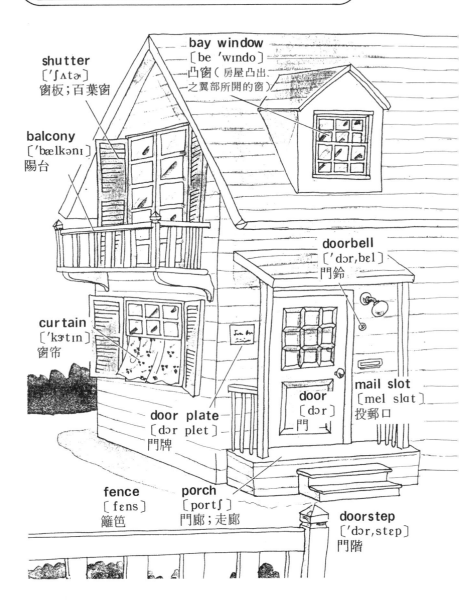

bay window
〔be 'wɪndo〕
凸窗（房屋凸出
之翼部所開的窗）

shutter
〔'ʃʌtə〕
窗板；百葉窗

balcony
〔'bælkənɪ〕
陽台

doorbell
〔'dɔr,bɛl〕
門鈴

curtain
〔'kɜtɪn〕
窗帘

door plate
〔dɔr plet〕
門牌

door
〔dɔr〕
門

mail slot
〔mel slɑt〕
投郵口

fence
〔fɛns〕
籬笆

porch
〔portʃ〕
門廊；走廊

doorstep
〔'dɔr,stɛp〕
門階

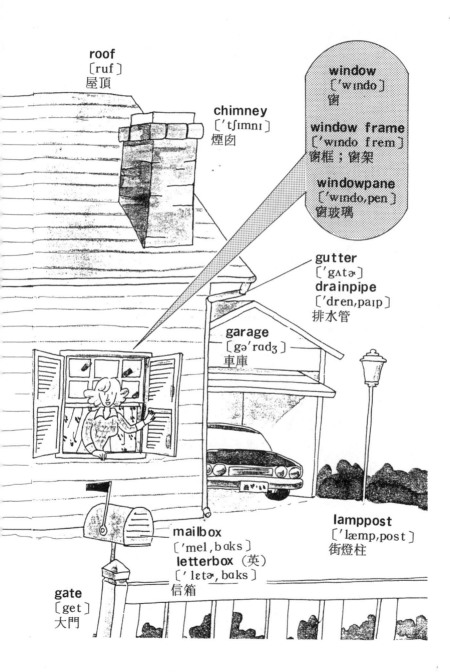

roof
〔ruf〕
屋頂

chimney
〔'tʃɪmnɪ〕
煙囪

window
〔'wɪndo〕
窗

window frame
〔'wɪndo frem〕
窗框；窗架

windowpane
〔'wɪndo,pen〕
窗玻璃

gutter
〔'gʌtɚ〕
drainpipe
〔'dren,paɪp〕
排水管

garage
〔gə'rɑdʒ〕
車庫

mailbox
〔'mel,bɑks〕
letterbox（英）
〔'lɛtɚ,bɑks〕
信箱

lamppost
〔'læmp,post〕
街燈柱

gate
〔get〕
大門

㉕ 花園　　*Garden*

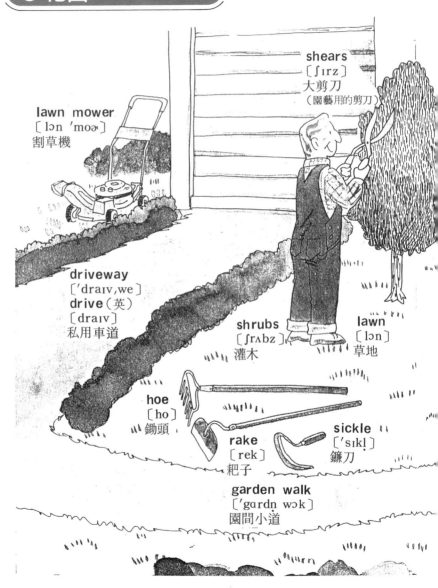

shears
〔ʃɪrz〕
大剪刀
（園藝用的剪刀）

lawn mower
〔lɔn ˈmoɚ〕
割草機

driveway
〔ˈdraɪˌwe〕
drive（英）
〔draɪv〕
私用車道

shrubs
〔ʃrʌbz〕
灌木

lawn
〔lɔn〕
草地

hoe
〔ho〕
鋤頭

rake
〔rek〕
耙子

sickle
〔ˈsɪkḷ〕
鐮刀

garden walk
〔ˈgɑrdn wɔk〕
園間小道

shovel
〔'ʃʌvl〕
鏟；鐵鍬

spade
〔sped〕
鋤

trowel
〔'trauəl〕
小鏟子

flowerbed
〔'flauɚ ˌbɛd〕
花壇；花床

watering can
〔'wɔtərɪŋ kæn〕
灑水壺

hose
〔hoz〕
水管

sprinkler
〔'sprɪŋklɚ〕
灑水裝置

㉖ 玄關　*Entrance*

wall
〔wɔl〕
牆；壁

step
〔stɛp〕
台階

stairs
〔stɛrz〕
階梯；樓梯

handrail
〔'hænd,rel〕
扶手；欄干

hallway
〔'hɔl,we〕
走廊

coat hanger
〔kot ˈhæŋɚ〕
掛衣鈎；衣架

door knocker
〔ˈdɔr ˈnɑkɚ〕
門環

doorknob
〔ˈdɔr,nɑb〕
門把

shoe horn
〔ʃu hɔrn〕
鞋拔

doormat
〔ˈdɔr ,mæt〕
擦鞋墊

umbrella stand
〔ʌmˈbrɛlə stænd〕
雨傘架

㉗客廳 *Living Room*

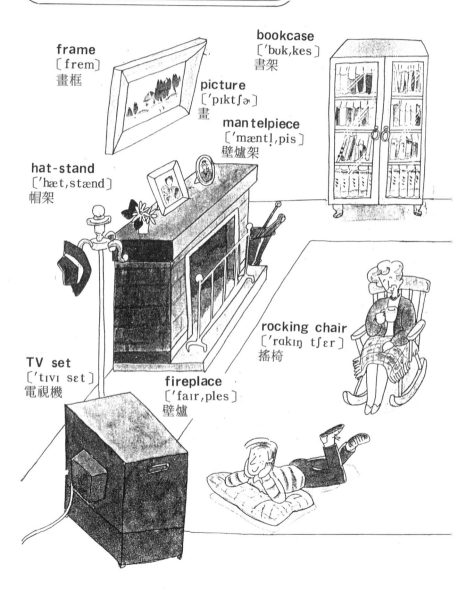

frame
〔frem〕
畫框

bookcase
〔'bʊk,kes〕
書架

picture
〔'pɪktʃɚ〕
畫

mantelpiece
〔'mæntḷ,pis〕
壁爐架

hat-stand
〔'hæt,stænd〕
帽架

rocking chair
〔'rɑkɪŋ tʃɛr〕
搖椅

TV set
〔'tivi sɛt〕
電視機

fireplace
〔'faɪr,ples〕
壁爐

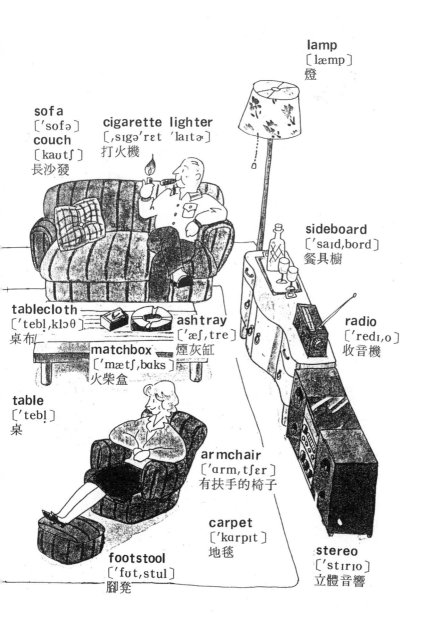

lamp
〔læmp〕
燈

sofa
〔'sofə〕
couch
〔kautʃ〕
長沙發

cigarette lighter
〔,sɪgə'rɛt 'laɪtə〕
打火機

sideboard
〔'saɪd,bord〕
餐具櫥

tablecloth
〔'tebḷ,klɔθ〕
桌布

ashtray
〔'æʃ,tre〕
煙灰缸

radio
〔'redɪ,o〕
收音機

matchbox
〔'mætʃ,bɑks〕
火柴盒

table
〔'tebḷ〕
桌

armchair
〔'ɑrm,tʃɛr〕
有扶手的椅子

carpet
〔'kɑrpɪt〕
地毯

footstool
〔'fʊt,stul〕
腳凳

stereo
〔'stɪrɪo〕
立體音響

㉘ 廚房　*Kitchen*

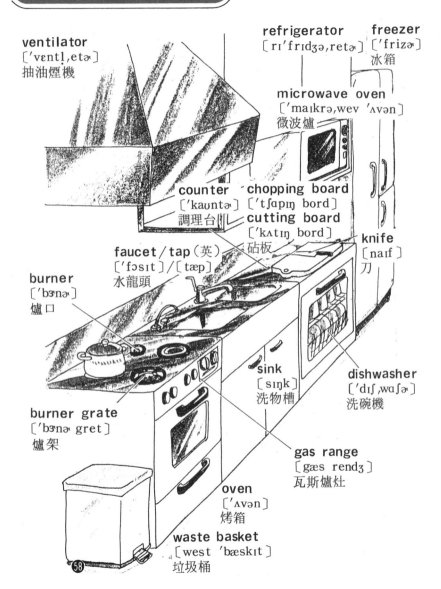

ventilator
〔'vɛntl,etə〕
抽油煙機

refrigerator
〔rɪ'frɪdʒə,retə〕
freezer
〔'frizə〕
冰箱

microwave oven
〔'maɪkrə,wev 'ʌvən〕
微波爐

counter
〔'kaʊntə〕
調理台

chopping board
〔'tʃɑpɪŋ bord〕
cutting board
〔'kʌtɪŋ bord〕
砧板

knife
〔naɪf〕
刀

faucet / tap（英）
〔'fɔsɪt〕/〔tæp〕
水龍頭

burner
〔'bɝnə〕
爐口

sink
〔sɪŋk〕
洗物槽

dishwasher
〔'dɪʃ,waʃə〕
洗碗機

burner grate
〔'bɝnə gret〕
爐架

gas range
〔gæs rendʒ〕
瓦斯爐灶

oven
〔'ʌvən〕
烤箱

waste basket
〔west 'bæskɪt〕
垃圾桶

58

vacuum bottle
〔ˈvækjuəm ˈbɑtl̩〕
熱水瓶

cupboard
〔ˈkʌbəd〕
碗櫥

drip coffee maker
〔drɪp ˈkɔfɪ ˈmekɚ〕
滴泡咖啡壺

toaster
〔ˈtostɚ〕
烤麵包機

cup
〔kʌp〕
杯

fork
〔fɔrk〕
叉

glass
〔glæs〕
玻璃杯

spoon
〔spun〕
匙

kettle
〔'kɛtḷ〕
壺

percolator
〔'pɚkə͵letɚ〕
咖啡壺

stock pot
〔stɑk pɑt〕
湯鍋

stew pot
〔stju pɑt〕
燉鍋

skillet
〔'skɪlɪt〕
frying pan
〔'fraɪŋ pæn〕
煎鍋

butter knife
〔'bʌtɚ naɪf〕
奶油刀

plate
〔plet〕
盤

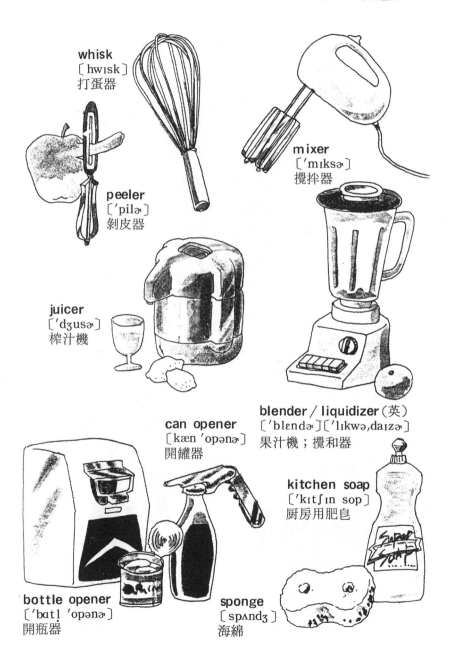

whisk
〔hwɪsk〕
打蛋器

peeler
〔'pilɚ〕
剝皮器

mixer
〔'mɪksɚ〕
攪拌器

juicer
〔'dʒusɚ〕
榨汁機

blender / liquidizer（英）
〔'blɛndɚ〕〔'lɪkwəˌdaɪzɚ〕
果汁機；攪和器

can opener
〔kæn 'opənɚ〕
開罐器

kitchen soap
〔'kɪtʃɪn sop〕
廚房用肥皂

bottle opener
〔'bɑtl 'opənɚ〕
開瓶器

sponge
〔spʌndʒ〕
海綿

㉙臥室　*Bedroom*

wardrobe
〔'wɔrd,rob〕
衣櫃

nightgown
〔'naɪt,gaʊn〕
睡袍

chest of drawers
〔tʃɛst əv drɔrz〕
五斗櫃

pajamas
〔pə'dʒæməz〕
睡衣

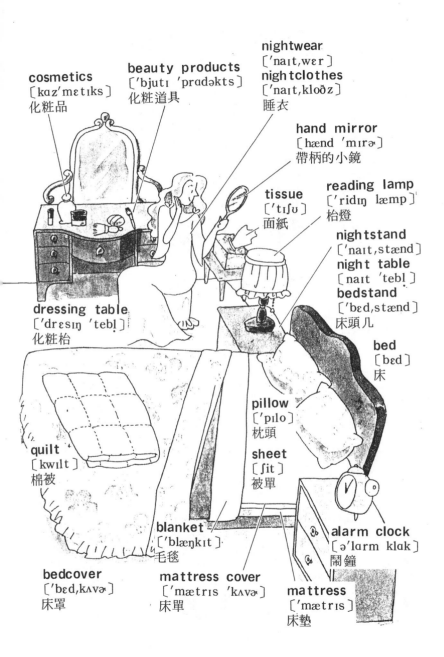

cosmetics
〔kɑz'mɛtɪks〕
化粧品

beauty products
〔'bjutɪ 'prɑdəkts〕
化粧道具

nightwear
〔'naɪt,wɛr〕
nightclothes
〔'naɪt,kloðz〕
睡衣

hand mirror
〔hænd 'mɪrə〕
帶柄的小鏡

tissue
〔'tɪʃʊ〕
面紙

reading lamp
〔'ridɪŋ læmp〕
枱燈

nightstand
〔'naɪt,stænd〕
night table
〔naɪt 'tebl〕
bedstand
〔'bɛd,stænd〕
床頭几

dressing table
〔'drɛsɪŋ 'tebl〕
化粧枱

bed
〔bɛd〕
床

quilt
〔kwɪlt〕
棉被

pillow
〔'pɪlo〕
枕頭

sheet
〔ʃit〕
被單

blanket
〔'blæŋkɪt〕
毛毯

alarm clock
〔ə'lɑrm klɑk〕
鬧鐘

bedcover
〔'bɛd,kʌvə〕
床罩

mattress cover
〔'mætrɪs 'kʌvə〕
床單

mattress
〔'mætrɪs〕
床墊

㉚嬰兒房　*Infant's Room*

stroller
〔'strolɚ〕
pushchair（英）
〔'pʌʃ,tʃɛr〕
嬰兒車

teething ring
〔'tiðɪŋ rɪŋ〕
（給長牙的嬰兒咬的）
象牙環

maternity dress
〔mə'tɝnətɪ drɛs〕
孕婦裝

rag doll
〔ræg dɑl〕
（用碎布做的）
玩偶

rattle
〔'rætl̩〕
撥浪鼓

walker
〔'wɔkɚ〕
學步車

cradle
〔'kredl̩〕
搖籃

dollhouse
〔'dɑl,haʊs〕
玩具房子

picture book
〔'pɪktʃɚ bʊk〕
畫本

building blocks
〔'bɪldɪŋ blɑks〕
積木

crayon
〔'kreən〕
蠟筆

doll
〔dɑl〕
洋娃娃

bunk bed
〔bʌŋk bɛd〕
雙層床

crib
〔krɪb〕
cot（英）
〔kɑt〕
嬰兒床

toy
〔tɔɪ〕
玩具

playpen
〔'ple͵pɛn〕
（為防止危險的）危欄

rocking horse
〔'rɑkɪŋ hɔrs〕
搖擺木馬

small chest of drawers
〔smɔl tʃɛst əv 'drɔəz〕
小五斗櫃

㉛ 浴室 *Bathroom*

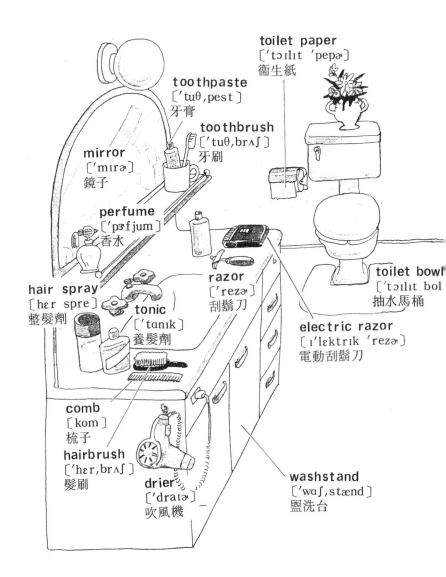

toilet paper
〔'tɔɪlɪt 'pepɚ〕
衛生紙

toothpaste
〔'tuθ,pest〕
牙膏

toothbrush
〔'tuθ,brʌʃ〕
牙刷

mirror
〔'mɪrɚ〕
鏡子

perfume
〔'pɝfjum〕
香水

razor
〔'rezɚ〕
刮鬍刀

toilet bowl
〔'tɔɪlɪt bol〕
抽水馬桶

hair spray
〔hɛr spre〕
整髮劑

tonic
〔'tanɪk〕
養髮劑

electric razor
〔ɪ'lɛktrɪk 'rezɚ〕
電動刮鬍刀

comb
〔kom〕
梳子

hairbrush
〔'hɛr,brʌʃ〕
髮刷

drier
〔'draɪɚ〕
吹風機

washstand
〔'waʃ,stænd〕
盥洗台

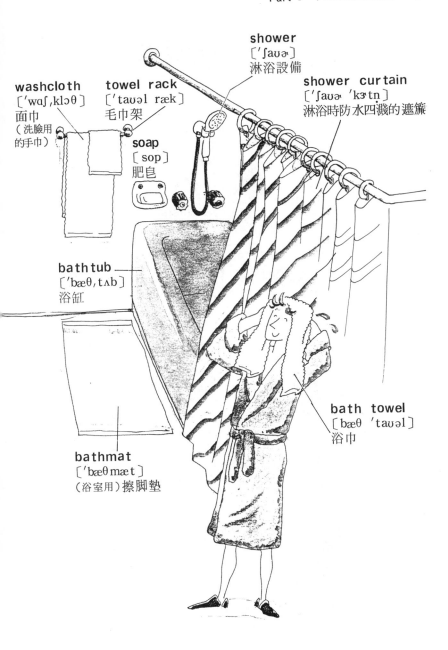

shower
〔'ʃauɚ〕
淋浴設備

shower curtain
〔'ʃauɚ 'kɝtn〕
淋浴時防水四濺的遮簾

washcloth
〔'waʃ,klɔθ〕
面巾
（洗臉用
的手巾）

towel rack
〔'tauəl ræk〕
毛巾架

soap
〔sop〕
肥皂

bathtub
〔'bæθ,tʌb〕
浴缸

bath towel
〔bæθ 'tauəl〕
浴巾

bathmat
〔'bæθ mæt〕
（浴室用）擦脚墊

㉜家事室　　*Utility Room*

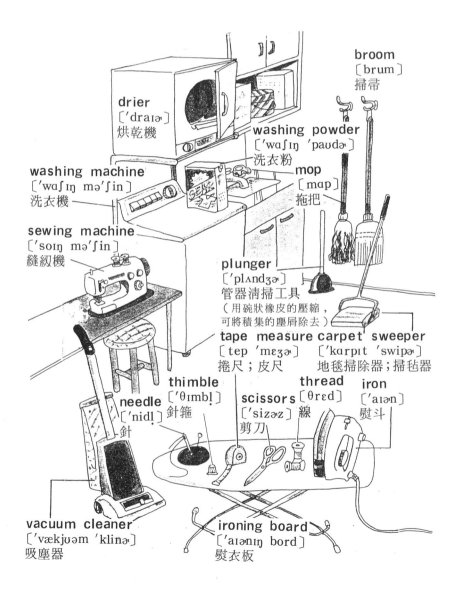

drier
〔'draɪə〕
烘乾機

washing machine
〔'waʃɪŋ mə'ʃin〕
洗衣機

sewing machine
〔'soɪŋ mə'ʃin〕
縫紉機

broom
〔brum〕
掃帚

washing powder
〔'waʃɪŋ 'paʊdə〕
洗衣粉

mop
〔map〕
拖把

plunger
〔'plʌndʒə〕
管器清掃工具
（用碗狀橡皮的壓縮，
可將積集的塵屑除去）

tape measure
〔tep 'mɛʒə〕
捲尺；皮尺

carpet sweeper
〔'karpɪt 'swipə〕
地毯掃除器；掃毡器

thimble
〔'θɪmbl̩〕
針箍

needle
〔'nidl̩〕
針

scissors
〔'sɪzəz〕
剪刀

thread
〔θrɛd〕
線

iron
〔'aɪən〕
熨斗

vacuum cleaner
〔'vækjʊəm 'klinə〕
吸塵器

ironing board
〔'aɪənɪŋ bord〕
熨衣板

Part 2

社會及文化

SOCIETY AND CULTURE

㉝世界各國　*Countries*

Asia
〔′eʃə〕
亞洲

Republic of China
〔rɪ′pʌblɪk əv tʃaɪnə〕
中華民國

Taipei
〔′taɪ′pe〕
台北

Philippines
〔′fɪlə,pinz〕
菲律賓

Manila
〔mə′nɪlə〕
馬尼拉

Indonesia
〔,ɪndo′niʃə〕
印尼共和國

Jakarta
〔dʒə′kɑrtə〕
雅加達

Singapore
〔′sɪŋgə,por〕
新加坡

Singapore
〔′sɪŋgə,por〕
新加坡

Thailand
〔′taɪlənd〕
泰國

Bangkok
〔′bæŋkɑk〕
曼谷

Vietnam
〔,viɛt′nɑm〕
越南

Hanoi
〔hɑ′nɔɪ〕
河內

Cambodia
〔kæm′bodɪə〕
高棉

Phnom Penh
〔′nɑm ′pɛn〕
金邊

India
〔′ɪndɪə〕
印度

New Delhi
〔nju′dɛlɪ〕
新德里

Iran
〔iˈrɑn〕
伊朗

Teheran
〔ˌtɛhəˈrɑn〕
德黑蘭

Iraq
〔iˈrɑk〕
伊拉克

Baghdad
〔ˈbægdæd〕
巴格達

Israel
〔ˈɪzrɪəl〕
以色列

Jerusalem
〔dʒəˈrusələm〕
耶路撒冷

Lebanon
〔ˈlɛbənən〕
黎巴嫩

Beirut
〔beˈrut〕
貝魯特

Syria
〔ˈsɪrɪə〕
敘利亞

Damascus
〔dəˈmæskəs〕
大馬士革

Saudi Arabia
〔səˈudɪ əˈrebɪə〕
沙烏地阿拉伯

Riyadh
〔rɪˈjɑd〕
利雅得

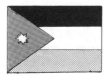

Jordan
〔ˈdʒɔrdn̩〕
約旦

Amman
〔æmˈmæn〕
阿曼

S. Korea
〔sɑʊθ koˈriə〕
南韓

Seoul
〔sol〕
漢城

N. Korea
〔nɔrθ koˈriə〕
北韓

Pyongyang
〔ˈpjʌŋˈjɑn〕
平壤

Egypt
〔ˈidʒɪpt〕
埃及

Libya
〔ˈlɪbɪə〕
利比亞

Africa
〔ˈæfrɪkə〕
非洲

Cairo
〔ˈkaɪro〕
開羅

Tripoli
〔ˈtrɪpəlɪ〕
的黎波里

Algeria
〔ælˈdʒɪrɪə〕
阿爾及利亞

Morocco
〔məˈrako〕
摩洛哥

Tunisia
〔tjuˈnɪʃɪə〕
突尼西亞

Algiers
〔ælˈdʒɪrz〕
阿爾及耳

Rabat
〔rəˈbat〕
拉巴特

Tunis
〔ˈtjunɪs〕
突尼斯

Ethiopia
〔ˌiθɪˈopɪə〕
衣索匹亞

Somalia
〔səˈmalɪə〕
索馬利亞

Kenya
〔ˈkɛnjə〕
肯亞

Addis Ababa
〔ˈædɪs ˈæbəbə〕
阿底斯阿貝巴

Mogadishu
〔ˌmagəˈdɪʃɪo〕
摩加底休

Nairobi
〔naɪˈrobɪ〕
奈洛比

Chad
〔tʃæd〕
查德

N'Djamena
〔ɛn'dʒɑmənə〕
恩將納

Angola
〔æŋ'golə〕
安古拉

Luanda
〔lu'ændə〕
羅安達

Tanzania
〔,tænzə'niə〕
坦尚尼亞

Dar es Salaam
〔'dɑr ɛs sə'lɑm〕
三蘭港

South Africa
〔sauθ 'æfɪkə〕
南非

Pretoria
〔prɪ'torɪə〕
普勒多利亞

Europe
〔'jurəp〕
歐洲

United Kingdom
〔ju'naɪtɪd 'kɪŋdəm〕
聯合王國

London
〔'lʌndən〕
倫敦

Ireland
〔'aɪrlənd〕
愛爾蘭

Dublin
〔'dʌblɪn〕
都柏林

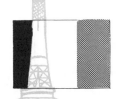

France
〔fræns〕
法國

Paris
〔'pærɪs〕
巴黎

Italy
〔'ɪtlɪ〕
義大利

Rome
〔rom〕
羅馬

Spain
〔spen〕
西班牙

Madrid
〔məˈdrɪd〕
馬德里

Portugal
〔ˈportʃəgḷ〕
葡萄牙

Lisbon
〔ˈlɪzbən〕
里斯本

Greece
〔gris〕
希臘

Athens
〔ˈæθənz〕
雅典

Netherlands
〔ˈnɛðələndz〕
尼德蘭

Amsterdam
〔ˈæmstɚˌdæm〕
阿姆斯特丹

Belgium
〔ˈbɛldʒɪəm〕
比利時

Brussels
〔ˈbrʌsḷz〕
布魯塞爾

Sweden
〔ˈswidn̩〕
瑞典

Stockholm
〔ˈstak,hom〕
斯德歌爾摩

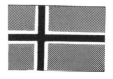

Norway
〔ˈnɔrwe〕
挪威

Oslo
〔ˈaslo〕
奧斯陸

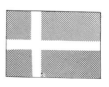

Denmark
〔ˈdɛnmɑrk〕
丹麥

Copenhagen
〔ˌkopənˈhegən〕
哥本哈根

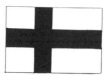

Finland
〔ˈfɪnlənd〕
芬蘭

Helsinki
〔ˈhɛlsɪŋkɪ〕
赫爾辛基

Luxemburg
〔'lʌksəm,bɝg〕
盧森堡

Luxemburg
〔'lʌksəm,bɝg〕
盧森堡

Germany
〔'dʒɝmənɪ〕
德國

Berlin
〔bɝ'lɪn〕
柏林

Poland
〔'polənd〕
波蘭

Warsaw
〔'wɔrsɔ〕
華沙

Rumania
〔ru'menɪə〕
羅馬尼亞

Bucharest
〔,bukə'rɛst〕
布加勒斯特

Hungary
〔'hʌngərɪ〕
匈牙利

Budapest
〔,bjudə'pɛst〕
布達佩斯

Bulgaria
〔bʊl'gɛrɪə〕
保加利亞

Sofia
〔so'fiə〕
索菲亞

Yugoslavia
〔,jugo'slɑvɪə〕
南斯拉夫

Belgrade
〔'bɛlgred〕
貝爾格勒

Czechoslovakia
〔'tʃɛkəslo'vækɪə〕
捷克斯拉夫共和國

Prague
〔preg〕
布拉格

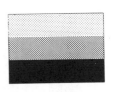

Russia
〔'rʌʃə〕
俄羅斯

Moscow
〔'mɑsko〕
莫斯科

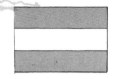

Switzerland
〔'swɪtsələnd〕
瑞士

Austria
〔'ɔstrɪə〕
奧地利

North and South America
〔nɔrθ ənd sauθ ə'mɛrɪkə〕
南北美洲

Bern
〔bɝn〕
伯恩

Vienna
〔vɪ'ɛnə〕
維也納

Canada
〔'kænədə〕
加拿大

United States
〔ju'naɪtɪd 'stets〕
美國

Cuba
〔'kjubə〕
古巴

Ottawa
〔'ɑtəwə〕
渥太華

Washington D.C.
〔'wɑʃɪŋtən di si〕
華盛頓

Havana
〔hə'vænə〕
哈瓦那

Mexico
〔'mɛksɪ,ko〕
墨西哥

El Salvador
〔ɛl 'sælvə,dɔr〕
薩爾瓦多

Nicaragua
〔,nɪkə'rɑgwə〕
尼加拉瓜

Mexico City
〔'mɛksɪ,ko 'sɪtɪ〕
墨西哥城

San Salvador
〔sæn'sælvə,dɔr〕
聖薩爾瓦多

Managua
〔mə'nɑgwə〕
馬拿瓜

sta Rica
[ˌɑstə ˈrikə]
斯大黎加

n José
[ˌsanhoˈsɛ]
約瑟

Colombia
[kəˈlʌmbɪə]
哥倫比亞

Bogota
[ˌbogəˈtɑ]
波哥大

Venezuela
[ˌvɛnəˈzwilə]
委內瑞拉

Caracas
[kɑˈrɑkɑs]
加拉卡斯

azil
[ˌrəˈzil]
西

asilia
[ˌrəˈziljə]
西利亞

Chile
[ˈtʃɪlɪ]
智利

Santiago
[ˌsæntɪˈɑgo]
聖地牙哥

Argentina
[ˌɑrdʒənˈtinə]
阿根廷

Buenos Aires
[ˈbwenɔs ˈaɪres]
布宜諾斯艾利斯

Oceania
[ˌoʃɪˈænɪə]
大洋洲（中南太
平洋諸島集合稱）

Australia
[ɔˈstreljə]
澳洲

Canberra
[ˈkænbərə]
坎培拉

New Zealand
[nju ˈzilənd]
紐西蘭

Wellington
[ˈwɛlɪŋtən]
威靈頓

㉞政治　*Politics*

Democracy
〔dəˈmɑkrəsɪ〕
民主政治

Legislature
〔ˈlɛdʒɪsˌletʃɚ〕
立法

separation of powers
〔ˌsɛpəˈreʃən əv ˈpauɚz〕
三權分立

Judiciary
〔dʒuˈdɪʃɪˌɛrɪ〕
司法

Executive
〔ɪgˈzɛkjutɪv〕
行政

Capitol Hill（美）
〔ˈkæpətl̩ hɪl〕
美國國會大廈
Congress（美）
〔ˈkɑŋgrəs〕
國會
The Senate（美）
〔ðə ˈsɛnɪt〕
參議院
Senator（美）
〔ˈsɛnətɚ〕
參議院議員
The House of Representives
〔ðə haus əv ˌrɛprɪˈzɛntətɪvz〕
衆議院（美）
Member of Congress（美）
〔ˈmɛmbɚ əv ˈkɑŋgrəs〕
衆議院議員

the House of Parliament（英）
〔ðə haus əv ˈpɑrləmənt〕
國會議事廳
Parliament（英）
〔ˈpɑrləmənt〕
國會
the House of Lords（英）
〔ðə haus əv lɔrdz〕
上院
Lord（英）
〔lɔrd〕
上院議員
the House of Commons（英）
〔ðə haus əv ˈkɑmənz〕
下院
Member of Parliament（英）
〔ˈmɛmbɚ əv ˈpɑrləmənt〕
下院議員

Chief Justice of the Supreme Court
〔tʃif ˈdʒʌstɪs əv ðə səˈprim kɔrt〕
最高法院院長

presiding judge
〔prɪˈzaɪdɪŋ dʒʌdʒ〕
審判長

judge
〔dʒʌdʒ〕
法官

presidential government
〔ˌprɛzəˈdɛnʃəl ˈgʌvənmənt〕
總統制

Administration（美）
〔ədˌmɪnəˈstreʃən〕
政府；內閣

President
〔ˈprɛzədənt〕
總統

Vice President
〔vaɪs ˈprɛzədənt〕
副總統

Secretary
〔ˈsɛkrəˌtɛrɪ〕
國務卿

constitutional monarchy（英）
〔ˌkɑnsəˈtjuʃənl̩ ˈmɑnəkɪ〕
君主政體

government（英）
〔ˈgʌvənmənt〕
政府

cabinet
〔ˈkæbənɪt〕
內閣

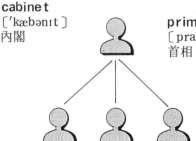

prime minister
〔praɪm ˈmɪnɪstɚ〕
首相；內閣總統

minister
〔ˈmɪnɪstɚ〕
部長

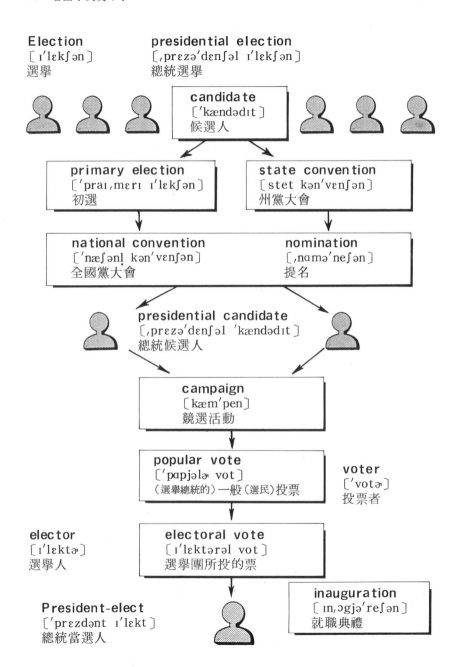

Election
〔ɪˈlɛkʃən〕
選舉

presidential election
〔ˌprɛzəˈdɛnʃəl ɪˈlɛkʃən〕
總統選舉

candidate
〔ˈkændədɪt〕
候選人

primary election
〔ˈpraɪˌmɛrɪ ɪˈlɛkʃən〕
初選

state convention
〔stet kənˈvɛnʃən〕
州黨大會

national convention
〔ˈnæʃənḷ kənˈvɛnʃən〕
全國黨大會

nomination
〔ˌnɑməˈneʃən〕
提名

presidential candidate
〔ˌprɛzəˈdɛnʃəl ˈkændədɪt〕
總統候選人

campaign
〔kæmˈpen〕
競選活動

popular vote
〔ˈpɑpjələ vot〕
（選舉總統的）一般（選民）投票

voter
〔ˈvotɚ〕
投票者

elector
〔ɪˈlɛktɚ〕
選舉人

electoral vote
〔ɪˈlɛktərəl vot〕
選舉團所投的票

President-elect
〔ˈprɛzdənt ɪˈlɛkt〕
總統當選人

inauguration
〔ɪnˌɔgjəˈreʃən〕
就職典禮

political party
〔pə'lɪtɪkḷ 'pɑrtɪ〕
政黨

Republican Party(美)
〔rɪ'pʌblɪkən 'pɑrtɪ〕
共和黨

Republican
〔rɪ'pʌblɪkən〕
共和黨員

Democratic Party(美)
〔ˌdɛmə'krætɪk 'pɑrtɪ〕
民主黨

Democrat
〔'dɛməˌkræt〕
民主黨員

Conservative Party(英)
〔kən'sɝvətɪv 'pɑrtɪ〕
保守黨

Labour Party(英)
〔'lebɚ 'pɑrtɪ〕
工黨

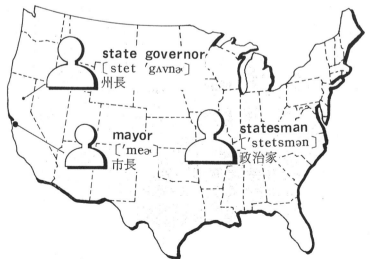

state governor
〔stet 'gʌvnɚ〕
州長

mayor
〔'meɚ〕
市長

statesman
〔'stetsmən〕
政治家

㉟農業　*Agriculture*

windmill
〔'wɪnd,mɪl〕
風車

pasture
〔'pæstʃɚ〕
牧場

rancher
〔'ræntʃɚ〕
農場主人；牧
場管理人

farmer
〔'fɑrmɚ〕
農場主；農夫

silo
〔'saɪlo〕
飼料貯藏庫

barn
〔bɑrn〕
穀倉

toolshed
〔'tul,ʃɛd〕
toolhouse
〔'tul,haʊs〕
堆放工具的小
屋（通常在房屋後）

stable
〔'stebḷ〕
馬廄

pigpen
〔'pɪg,pɛn〕
豬欄；豬圈

chicken house
〔'tʃɪkɪn haʊs〕
養雞場

field
〔fild〕
田地

cornfield
〔'kɔrn,fild〕
麥田；稻田；玉米田

vegetable garden
〔'vɛdʒətəbl 'gɑrdn̩〕
菜園

seeder
〔'sidɚ〕
播種機

manure
〔mə'njur〕
肥料；糞

feed
〔fid〕
飼料

tractor
〔'træktɚ〕
牽引機；拖曳機

hay
〔he〕
乾草

bale loader
〔bel 'lodɚ〕
打包裝貨機

cultivator
〔'kʌltə,vetɚ〕
鬆土除草機

combine
〔'kɑmbaɪn〕
聯合收割打穀機

㊱ 工業 *Industry*

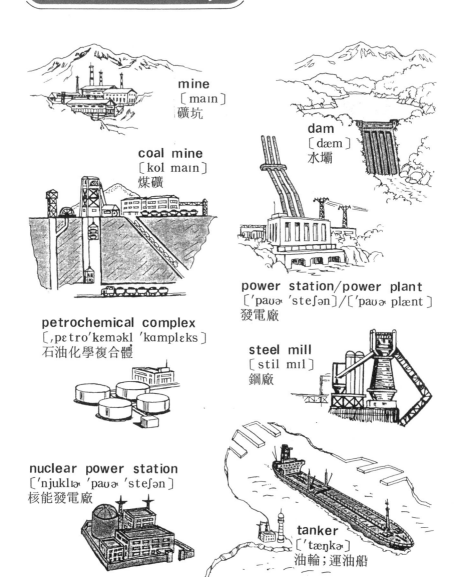

mine
〔maɪn〕
礦坑

dam
〔dæm〕
水壩

coal mine
〔kol maɪn〕
煤礦

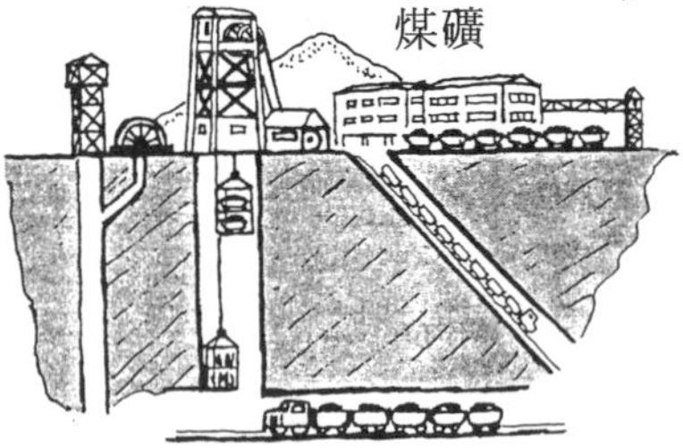

power station/power plant
〔'paʊɚ 'steʃən〕/〔'paʊɚ plænt〕
發電廠

petrochemical complex
〔ˌpɛtro'kɛməkl 'kɑmplɛks〕
石油化學複合體

steel mill
〔stil mɪl〕
鋼廠

nuclear power station
〔'njuklɪɚ 'paʊɚ 'steʃən〕
核能發電廠

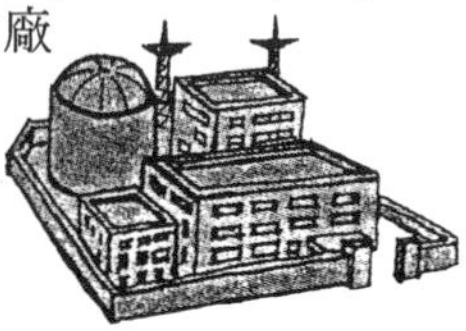

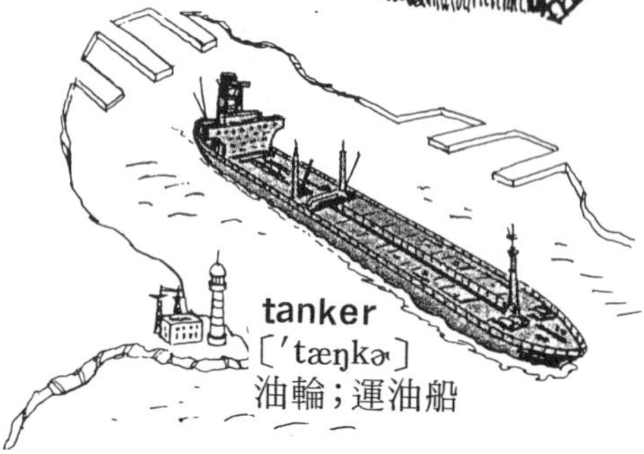

tanker
〔'tæŋkɚ〕
油輪；運油船

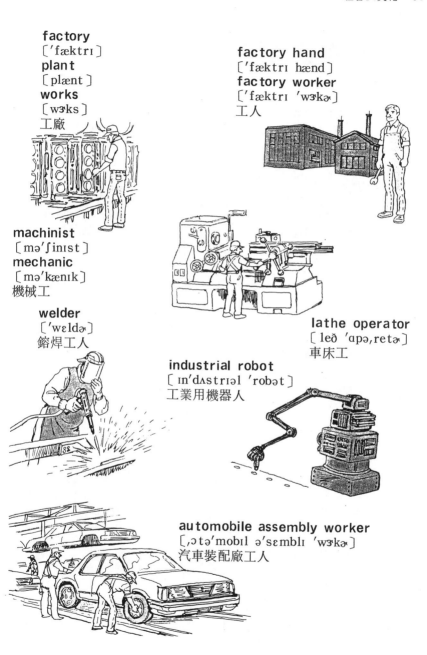

factory
〔'fæktrɪ〕
plant
〔plænt〕
works
〔wɝks〕
工廠

factory hand
〔'fæktrɪ hænd〕
factory worker
〔'fæktrɪ 'wɝkɚ〕
工人

machinist
〔mə'ʃɪnɪst〕
mechanic
〔mə'kænɪk〕
機械工

welder
〔'wɛldɚ〕
鎔焊工人

lathe operator
〔leð 'ɑpə,retɚ〕
車床工

industrial robot
〔ɪn'dʌstrɪəl 'robət〕
工業用機器人

automobile assembly worker
〔,ɔtə'mobɪl ə'sɛmblɪ 'wɝkɚ〕
汽車裝配廠工人

(37) 商業 *Commerce*

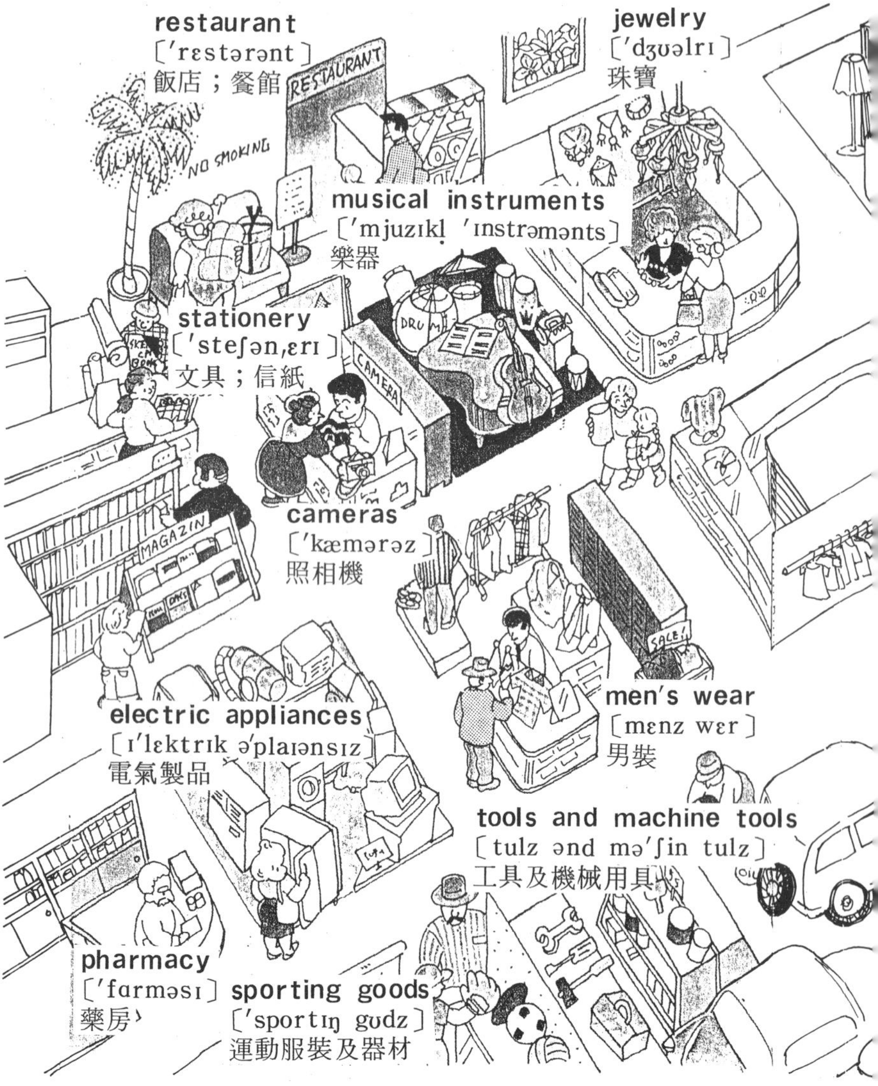
restaurant
〔ˈrɛstərənt〕
飯店；餐館
RESTAURANT
NO SMOKING
jewelry
〔ˈdʒʊəlrɪ〕
珠寶
musical instruments
〔ˈmjuzɪkḷ ˈɪnstrəmənts〕
樂器
DRUM
stationery
〔ˈsteʃən,ɛrɪ〕
文具；信紙
CAMERA
cameras
〔ˈkæmərəz〕
照相機
MAGAZIN
SALE!
men's wear
〔mɛnz wɛr〕
男裝
electric appliances
〔ɪˈlɛktrɪk əˈplaɪənsɪz〕
電氣製品
tools and machine tools
〔tulz ənd məˈʃin tulz〕
工具及機械用具
pharmacy
〔ˈfɑrməsɪ〕
藥房
sporting goods
〔ˈsportɪŋ gʊdz〕
運動服裝及器材

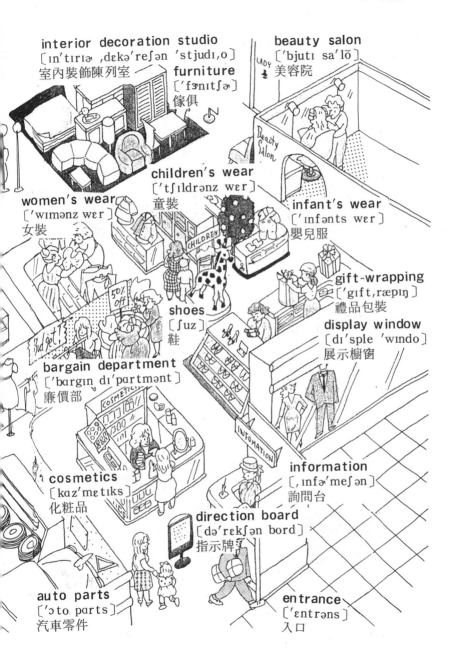

interior decoration studio
〔ɪnˈtɪrɪə ˌdɛkəˈreʃən ˈstjudɪˌo〕
室內裝飾陳列室

furniture
〔ˈfɝnɪtʃə〕
傢俱

beauty salon
〔ˈbjutɪ saˈlõ〕
美容院

children's wear
〔ˈtʃɪldrənz wɛr〕
童裝

women's wear
〔ˈwɪmənz wɛr〕
女裝

infant's wear
〔ˈɪnfənts wɛr〕
嬰兒服

gift-wrapping
〔ˈgɪftˌræpɪŋ〕
禮品包裝

shoes
〔ʃuz〕
鞋

display window
〔dɪˈsple ˈwɪndo〕
展示櫥窗

bargain department
〔ˈbɑrgɪn dɪˈpɑrtmənt〕
廉價部

cosmetics
〔kɑzˈmɛtɪks〕
化粧品

information
〔ˌɪnfəˈmeʃən〕
詢問台

direction board
〔dəˈrɛkʃən bord〕
指示牌

auto parts
〔ˈɔto pɑrts〕
汽車零件

entrance
〔ˈɛntrəns〕
入口

㊳ 銀行　　　*Bank*

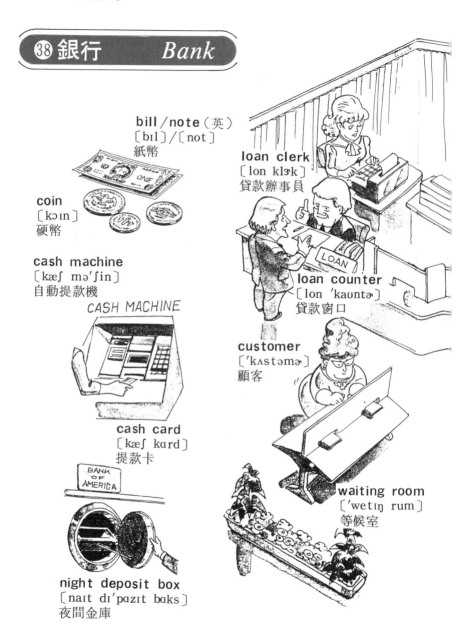

bill / note（英）
〔bɪl〕/〔not〕
紙幣

coin
〔kɔɪn〕
硬幣

cash machine
〔kæʃ məˈʃɪn〕
自動提款機

CASH MACHINE

cash card
〔kæʃ kɑrd〕
提款卡

BANK OF AMERICA

night deposit box
〔naɪt dɪˈpɑzɪt bɑks〕
夜間金庫

loan clerk
〔lon klɝk〕
貸款辦事員

LOAN

loan counter
〔lon ˈkaʊntɚ〕
貸款窗口

customer
〔ˈkʌstəmɚ〕
顧客

waiting room
〔ˈwetɪŋ rum〕
等候室

manager
〔'mænɪdʒɚ〕
經理

vault
〔vɔlt〕
保險箱

administrator
〔əd'mɪnə,stretɚ〕
主管

bank clerk
〔bæŋk klɝk〕
銀行職員

credit controller
〔'krɛdɪt kən'trolɚ〕
信用調查員

depositing and withdrawing money window
〔dɪ'pɑzɪtɪŋ ənd wɪð'drɔɪŋ 'mʌnɪ 'wɪndo〕
存提款窗口

cashier's window
〔kæ'ʃɪrz 'wɪndo〕
出納窗口

bankbook
〔'bæŋk,bʊk〕
passbook
〔'pæs,bʊk〕
存摺

personal check
〔'pɝsənl tʃɛk〕
個人支票

foreign exchange teller
〔'fɔrɪn ɪks'tʃendʒ 'tɛlɚ〕
外幣兌換員

㊴公司 *Company*

employer
〔ɪm'plɔɪə〕
雇用者
management
〔'mænɪdʒmənt〕
經理；管理人員

chairman
〔'tʃɛrmən〕
董事長

director
〔də'rɛktə〕
董事
president
〔'prɛzədənt〕
總經理；社長
vice president
〔vaɪs 'prɛzədənt〕
副總經理；副社長
senior managing director
〔'sinjə 'mænɪdʒɪŋ də'rɛktə〕
執行常務董事
managing director
〔'mænɪdʒɪŋ də'rɛktə〕
常務董事

controller
〔kən'trolə〕
監事

executive
〔ɪg'zɛkjʊtɪv〕
主管

personnel manager
〔ˌpɝsn'ɛl 'mænɪdʒə〕
人事部經理

finance manager
〔fə'næns 'mænɪdʒə〕
財務部經理

accounting manager
〔ə'kaʊntɪŋ 'mænɪdʒə〕
會計部經理

production manager
〔prə'dʌkʃən 'mænɪdʒə〕
生產部經理

marketing manager
〔'markɪtɪŋ 'mænɪdʒə〕
業務部經理

department manager
〔dɪ'partmənt 'mænɪdʒə〕
經理

assistant manager
〔ə'sɪstənt 'mænɪdʒə〕
副理

section manager
〔'sɛkʃən 'mænɪdʒə〕
課長

employee
〔ˌɛmplɔɪ'i〕
職員

labor
〔'lebə〕
勞工

labor union
〔'lebə 'junjən〕
工會

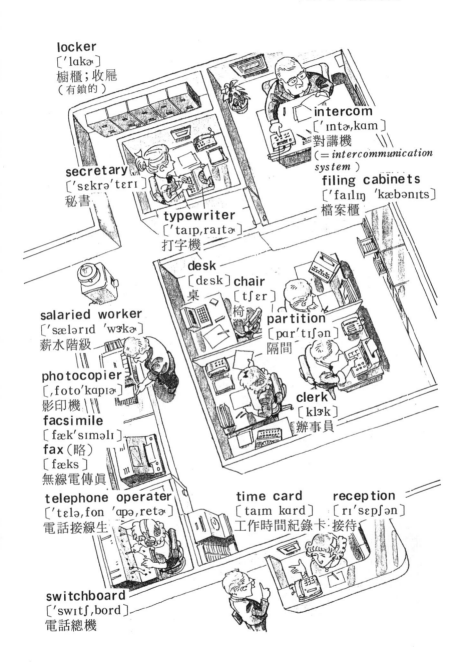

locker
〔'lakə〕
櫥櫃；收屜
（有鎖的）

intercom
〔'ɪntə,kɑm〕
對講機
（= *intercommunication system*）

filing cabinets
〔'faɪlɪŋ 'kæbənɪts〕
檔案櫃

secretary
〔'sɛkrə'tɛrɪ〕
秘書

typewriter
〔'taɪp,raɪtə〕
打字機

desk
〔dɛsk〕
桌

chair
〔tʃɛr〕
椅

partition
〔par'tɪʃən〕
隔間

salaried worker
〔'sælərɪd 'wɝkə〕
薪水階級

photocopier
〔,foto'kapɪə〕
影印機

facsimile
〔fæk'sɪməlɪ〕
fax（略）
〔fæks〕
無線電傳眞

clerk
〔klɝk〕
辦事員

telephone operater
〔'tɛlə,fon 'apə,retə〕
電話接線生

time card
〔taɪm kard〕
工作時間紀錄卡

reception
〔rɪ'sɛpʃən〕
接待

switchboard
〔'swɪtʃ,bord〕
電話總機

㊵郵局 *Post Office*

central post office
〔'sɛntrəl post 'ɑfɪs〕
中央郵局

postal clerk
〔'post̞l kl₃ˋk〕
郵局職員

stamp machine
〔stæmp mə'ʃin〕
郵票自動販賣機

mailman
〔'mel,mæn〕
postman（英）
〔'postmən〕
郵差

mail truck
〔mel trʌk〕
mail van（英）
〔mel væn〕
郵車

post-office box
〔'post ,ɔfɪs bɑks〕
P.O. Box（略）
郵政信箱

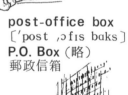

mailbox
〔'mel,bɑks〕
postbox
〔'post,bɑks〕
pillar-box（英）
〔'pɪlɚ,bɑks〕
郵筒

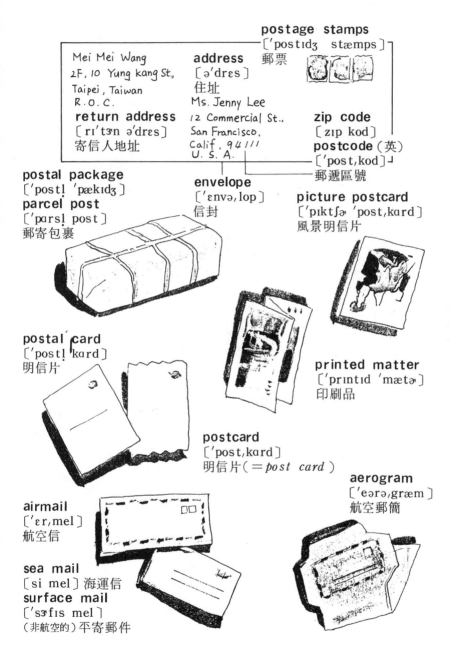

postage stamps
['postɪdʒ stæmps]
郵票

Mei Mei Wang
2F, 10 Yung kang St.,
Taipei, Taiwan
R.O.C.

address
[ə'drɛs]
住址

return address
[rɪ't3n ə'drɛs]
寄信人地址

Ms. Jenny Lee
12 Commercial St.,
San Francisco,
Calif, 94111
U.S.A.

zip code
[zɪp kod]

postcode (英)
['post,kod]
郵遞區號

postal package
['postl 'pækɪdʒ]
parcel post
['parsl post]
郵寄包裹

envelope
['ɛnvə,lop]
信封

picture postcard
['pɪktʃə 'post,kard]
風景明信片

postal card
['postl 'kard]
明信片

printed matter
['prɪntɪd 'mætə]
印刷品

postcard
['post,kard]
明信片 (= post card)

aerogram
['eərə,græm]
航空郵簡

airmail
['ɛr,mel]
航空信

sea mail
[si mel] 海運信
surface mail
['s3fɪs mel]
(非航空的)平寄郵件

㉑ 電話及電報　*Telephone and Telegram*

dial desk phone
〔'daɪəl dɛsk fon〕
撥號式電話

touch-tone desk phone
〔'tʌtʃ,ton dɛsk fon〕
按鍵式電話

telephone booth
〔'tɛlə,fon buθ〕
telephone kiosk (英)
〔'tɛlə,fon kɪ'ɑsk〕
公共電話亭

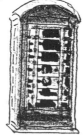

telephone directory
〔'tɛlə,fon də'rɛktərɪ〕
電話簿

pay phone
〔pe fon〕
public telephone
〔'pʌblɪk 'tɛlə,fon〕
公用電話

classified directory
〔'klæsə,faɪd də'rɛktərɪ〕
Yellow Pages
〔'jɛlo 'pedʒɪz〕
分類電話簿

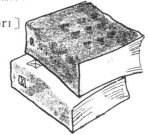

operator
〔'ɑpə,retə〕
接線生

telegram
〔'tɛlə,græm〕
電報

general directory
〔'dʒɛnərəl də'rɛktərɪ〕
家庭用電話簿

local call
〔'lokl̩ kɔl〕
市內電話

long-distance call
〔'lɔŋ 'dɪstəns kɔl〕
長途電話

international call
〔,ɪntɚ'næʃənl̩ kɔl〕
國際電話

81 - 3 - 123 - 4567

country code	**area code**	**city code**	**telephone number**
〔'kʌntrɪ kod〕	〔'ɛrɪə kod〕	〔'sɪtɪ kod〕	〔'tɛlə,fon 'nʌmbɚ〕
國際號碼	區域號碼	市內號碼	電話號碼

station-to-station call
〔'steʃən tə'steʃən kɔl〕
叫號長途電話

(内線)7777

person-to-person call
〔'pɝsən tə'pɝsən kɔl〕
叫人電話

● **collect call**
〔kə'lɛkt kɔl〕
reverse charge call
〔rɪ'vɝs tʃɑrdʒ kɔl〕
對方付費電話

extension
〔ɪk'stɛnʃən〕
分機
(英)

㊷警察　　*Police*

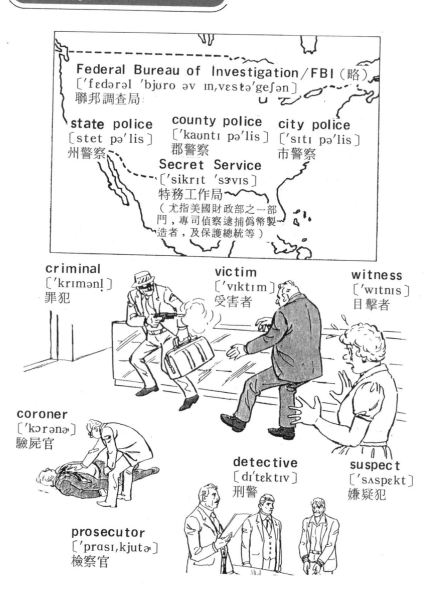

Federal Bureau of Investigation／FBI（略）
〔ˈfɛdərəl ˈbjʊro əv ɪnˌvɛstəˈgeʃən〕
聯邦調查局

state police
〔stet pəˈlis〕
州警察

county police
〔ˈkaʊntɪ pəˈlis〕
郡警察

city police
〔ˈsɪtɪ pəˈlis〕
市警察

Secret Service
〔ˈsikrɪt ˈsɝvɪs〕
特務工作局
（尤指美國財政部之一部
門，專司偵察逮捕偽幣製
造者，及保護總統等）

criminal
〔ˈkrɪmənl〕
罪犯

victim
〔ˈvɪktɪm〕
受害者

witness
〔ˈwɪtnɪs〕
目擊者

coroner
〔ˈkɔrənə〕
驗屍官

detective
〔dɪˈtɛktɪv〕
刑警

suspect
〔ˈsʌspɛkt〕
嫌疑犯

prosecutor
〔ˈprɑsɪˌkjutə〕
檢察官

uniform
〔'junə,fɔrm〕
制服

bulletproof vest
〔'bʊlɪt,pruf vɛst〕
防彈衣

gun
〔gʌn〕
鎗

holster
〔'holstɚ〕
手鎗皮套

bullets
〔'bʊlɪts〕
子彈

police officer
〔pə'lis 'ɔfəsɚ〕
cop（略）
〔kɑp〕
警官

police badge
〔pə'lis bædʒ〕
警徽

walkie-talkie
〔'wɔkɪ,tɔkɪ〕
手提無線電話機

handcuffs
〔'hænd,kʌfs〕
手銬

whistle
〔'hwɪsl̩〕
哨子

nightstick
〔'naɪt,stɪk〕
truncheon（英）
〔'trʌntʃən〕
警棒

highway patrol
〔'haɪ,we pə'trol〕
公路巡邏隊

police car
〔pə'lis kɑr〕
警車

㊸消防隊　*Fire Department*

helmet
〔ˈhɛlmɪt〕
鋼盔

fire·fighter
〔faɪr ˈfaɪtɚ〕
消防隊員

pick pole
〔pɪk pol〕
消防鉤；鷹嘴鉤

turnout coat
〔ˈtɝnˌaʊt kot〕
消防服

wrecking bar
〔ˈrɛkɪŋ bɑr〕
大型鐵鉗

glove
〔glʌv〕
手套

fire extinguisher
〔faɪr ɪkˈstɪŋgwɪʃɚ〕
滅火器

ax(e)
〔æks〕
斧

rope hose
〔rop hoz〕
消防用繩索

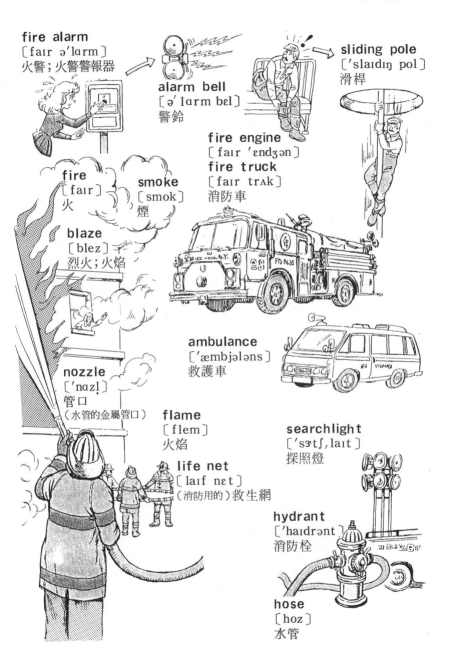

fire alarm
〔faɪr əˈlɑrm〕
火警;火警警報器

alarm bell
〔əˈlɑrm bɛl〕
警鈴

sliding pole
〔ˈslaɪdɪŋ pol〕
滑桿

fire engine
〔faɪr ˈɛndʒən〕
fire truck
〔faɪr trʌk〕
消防車

fire
〔faɪr〕
火

smoke
〔smok〕
煙

blaze
〔blez〕
烈火;火焰

nozzle
〔ˈnɑzl̩〕
管口
(水管的金屬管口)

ambulance
〔ˈæmbjələns〕
救護車

flame
〔flem〕
火焰

life net
〔laɪf nɛt〕
(消防用的)救生網

searchlight
〔ˈsɝtʃˌlaɪt〕
探照燈

hydrant
〔ˈhaɪdrənt〕
消防栓

hose
〔hoz〕
水管

㊸軍隊 *The Military*

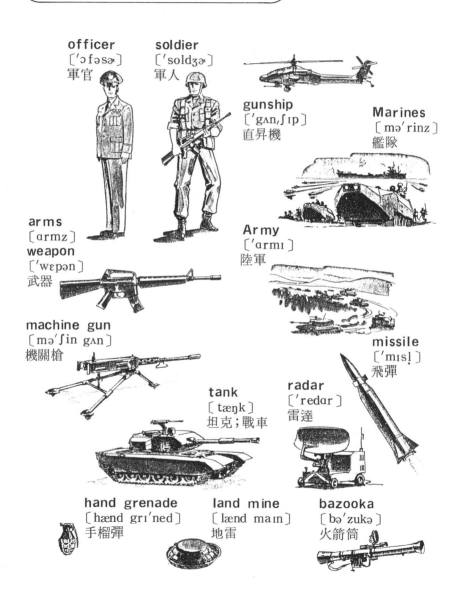

officer
〔ˈɔfəsə〕
軍官

soldier
〔ˈsoldʒə〕
軍人

gunship
〔ˈgʌnˌʃɪp〕
直昇機

Marines
〔məˈrinz〕
艦隊

arms
〔ɑrmz〕
weapon
〔ˈwɛpən〕
武器

Army
〔ˈɑrmɪ〕
陸軍

machine gun
〔məˈʃin gʌn〕
機關槍

missile
〔ˈmɪsl̩〕
飛彈

tank
〔tæŋk〕
坦克;戰車

radar
〔ˈredɑr〕
雷達

hand grenade
〔hænd grɪˈned〕
手榴彈

land mine
〔lænd maɪn〕
地雷

bazooka
〔bəˈzukə〕
火箭筒

Air Force
〔ɛr fɔrs〕
空軍

spy satellite
〔spaɪ ˈsætlˌaɪt〕
偵察衛星

bomber
〔ˈbɑmɚ〕
轟炸機

fighter
〔ˈfaɪtɚ〕
戰鬥機

military air transport
〔ˈmɪlə,tɛrɪ ɛr ˈtrænsport〕
軍用運輸機

nuclear weapon
〔ˈnjuklɪɚ ˈwɛpən〕
核子武器

navy
〔ˈnevɪ〕
海軍
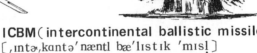

ICBM(intercontinental ballistic missile)
〔,ɪntɚ,kɑntəˈnæntl̩ bæˈlɪstɪk ˈmɪsl̩〕
洲際彈道飛彈

atomic bomb
〔əˈtɑmɪk bɑm〕
原子彈

warship
〔ˈwɔr,ʃɪp〕
軍艦

battleship
〔ˈbætl̩,ʃɪp〕
戰艦

hydrogen bomb
〔ˈhaɪdrədʒən bɑm〕
氫彈

aircraft carrier
〔ˈɛr,kræft ˈkærɪɚ〕
航空母艦
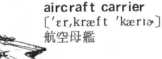

neutron bomb
〔ˈnjutrɑn bɑm〕
中子彈
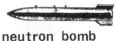

submarine
〔ˈsʌbmə,rin〕
潛水艇

torpedo
〔tɔrˈpido〕
魚雷

mine
〔maɪn〕
水雷；地雷

㊺醫院　*Hospital*

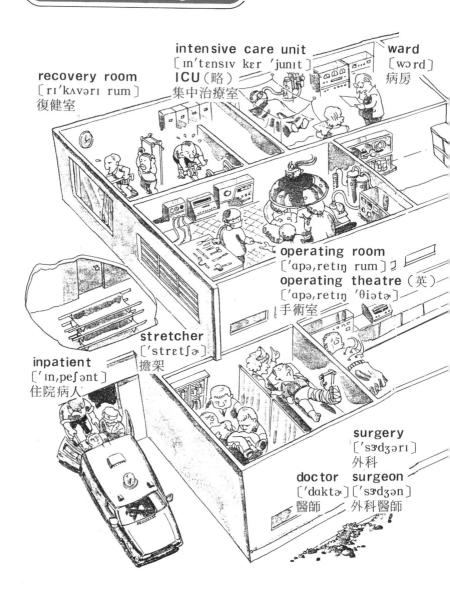

intensive care unit
〔ɪn'tɛnsɪv kɛr 'junɪt〕
ICU（略）
集中治療室

ward
〔wɔrd〕
病房

recovery room
〔rɪ'kʌvərɪ rum〕
復健室

operating room
〔'ɑpə,retɪŋ rum〕ㄖ
operating theatre（英）
〔'ɑpə,retɪŋ 'θɪətə〕
手術室

stretcher
〔'strɛtʃə〕
擔架

inpatient
〔'ɪn,peʃənt〕
住院病人

surgery
〔'sɝdʒərɪ〕
外科

doctor
〔'dɑktə〕
醫師

surgeon
〔'sɝdʒən〕
外科醫師

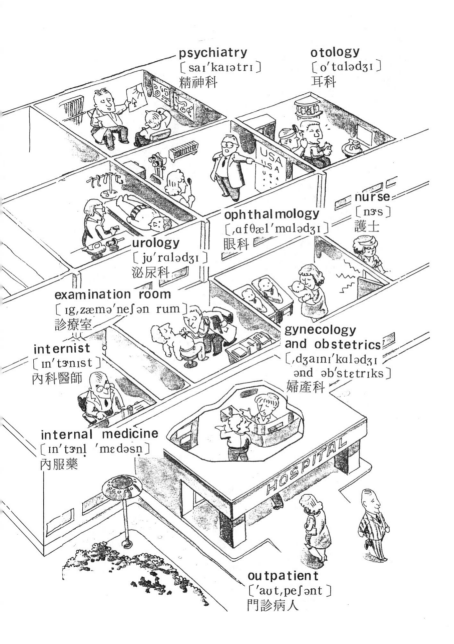

psychiatry
〔 saɪ'kaɪətrɪ 〕
精神科

otology
〔 o'tɑlədʒɪ 〕
耳科

ophthalmology
〔 ,ɑfθæl'mɑlədʒɪ 〕
眼科

nurse
〔 nɝs 〕
護士

urology
〔 jʊ'rɑlədʒɪ 〕
泌尿科

examination room
〔 ɪg,zæmə'neʃən rum 〕
診療室

internist
〔 ɪn'tɝnɪst 〕
內科醫師

gynecology and obstetrics
〔 ,dʒaɪnɪ'kɑlədʒɪ ənd əb'stɛtrɪks 〕
婦產科

internal medicine
〔 ɪn'tɝnl̩ 'mɛdəsn̩ 〕
內服藥

outpatient
〔 'aʊt,peʃənt 〕
門診病人

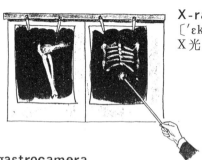

X-ray picture
〔'ɛks're 'pɪktʃə〕
X光片

wheelchair
〔'hwil'tʃɛr〕
輪椅

gastrocamera
〔gæstro'kæmərə〕
胃內視鏡

medicine
〔'mɛdəsn̩〕
藥

stethoscope
〔'stɛθə,skop〕
聽診器

syringe
〔'sɪrɪndʒ〕
注射器

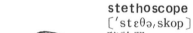

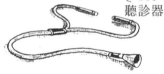

computerized axial tomography
〔kəm'pjutə,raɪzd 'æksɪəl to'mɑgrəfɪ〕
CAT（略）
電腦軸性斷層攝影術

thermometer
〔θə'mɑmətə〕
體溫計

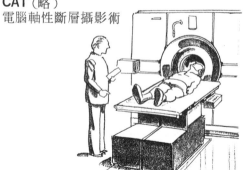

㊻ 學校　*Schools*

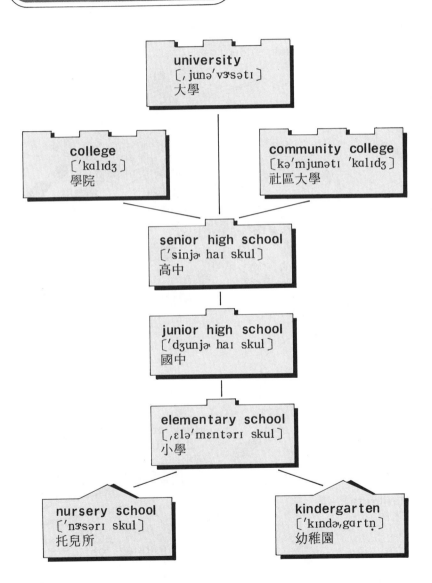

㊼大學校園　*Campus*

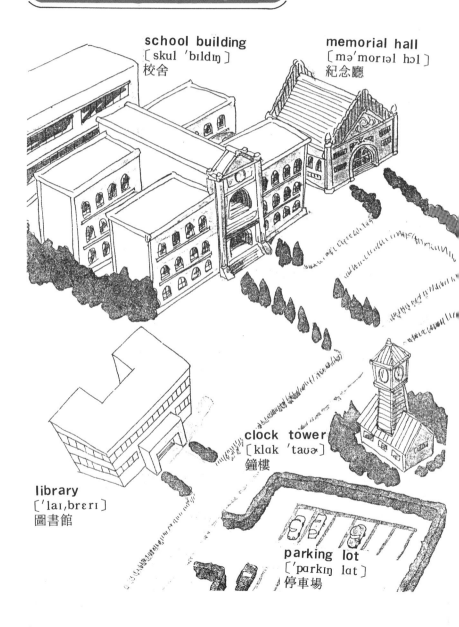

school building
〔skul ˈbɪldɪŋ〕
校舍

memorial hall
〔məˈmorɪəl hɔl〕
紀念廳

clock tower
〔klɑk ˈtauɚ〕
鐘樓

library
〔ˈlaɪˌbrɛrɪ〕
圖書館

parking lot
〔ˈpɑrkɪŋ lɑt〕
停車場

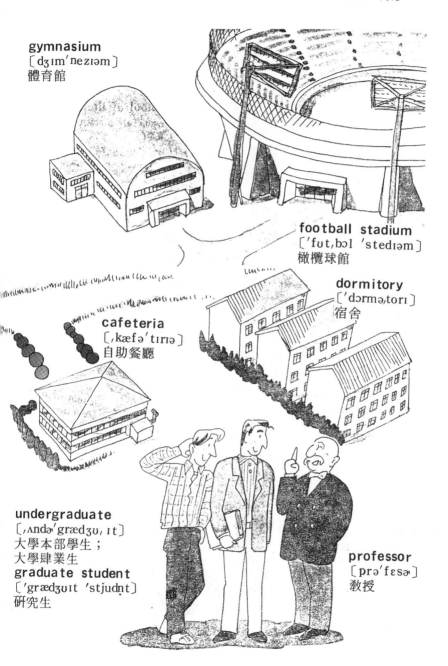

gymnasium
〔dʒɪmˈnezɪəm〕
體育館

football stadium
〔ˈfʊtˌbɔl ˈstedɪəm〕
橄欖球館

dormitory
〔ˈdɔrməˌtorɪ〕
宿舍

cafeteria
〔ˌkæfəˈtɪrɪə〕
自助餐廳

undergraduate
〔ˌʌndəˈgrædʒʊˌɪt〕
大學本部學生；
大學肄業生
graduate student
〔ˈgrædʒʊɪt ˈstjudn̩t〕
研究生

professor
〔prəˈfɛsə〕
教授

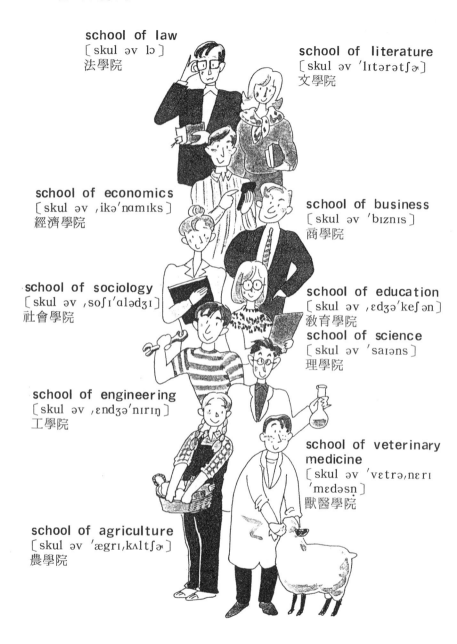

school of law
〔skul əv lɔ〕
法學院

school of literature
〔skul əv ˈlɪtərətʃɚ〕
文學院

school of economics
〔skul əv ˌikəˈnɑmɪks〕
經濟學院

school of business
〔skul əv ˈbɪznɪs〕
商學院

school of sociology
〔skul əv ˌsoʃɪˈɑlədʒɪ〕
社會學院

school of education
〔skul əv ˌɛdʒəˈkeʃən〕
教育學院

school of science
〔skul əv ˈsaɪəns〕
理學院

school of engineering
〔skul əv ˌɛndʒəˈnɪrɪŋ〕
工學院

school of veterinary
medicine
〔skul əv ˈvɛtrəˌnɛrɪ
ˈmɛdəsn̩〕
獸醫學院

school of agriculture
〔skul əv ˈægrɪˌkʌltʃɚ〕
農學院

school of pharmacy
〔skul əv ˈfɑrməsɪ〕
藥學院

school of dentistry
〔skuləv ˈdɛntɪstrɪ〕
牙醫學院

school of art
〔skul əv ɑrt〕
藝術學院

school of medicine
〔skul əv ˈmɛdəsṇ〕
醫學院

class
〔klæs ; klɑs〕
上課

lecture
〔ˈlɛktʃɚ〕
講課

textbook
〔ˈtɛkstˌbʊk〕
課本
notebook
〔ˈnotˌbʊk〕
筆記本

examination
〔ɪgˌzæməˈneʃən〕
exam（略）
〔ɪgˈzæm〕
考試

㊽各行各業 *Vocation*

farmer
〔ˈfɑrmɚ〕
農夫

fisherman
〔ˈfɪʃəmən〕
漁夫

teacher
〔ˈtitʃɚ〕
老師

cowboy
〔ˈkaʊˌbɔɪ〕
牛仔

architect
〔ˈɑrkəˌtɛkt〕
建築師

construction worker
〔kənˈstrʌkʃən ˈwɝkɚ〕
建築工人

carpenter
〔ˈkɑrpəntɚ〕
木匠

diplomat
〔ˈdɪpləˌmæt〕
外交官

translator
〔trænsˈletɚ〕
翻譯家；譯者

lawyer
〔ˈlɔjɚ〕
律師

reporter
〔rɪˋportɚ〕
記者

editor
〔ˋɛdɪtɚ〕
編輯

announcer
〔əˋnaʊnsɚ〕
廣播員

scientist
〔ˋsaɪəntɪst〕
科學家

TV producer
〔ti vi prəˋdjusɚ〕
電視製作人

computer engineer
〔kəmˋpjutɚ ˏɛndʒəˋnɪr〕
電腦工程師

photographer
〔fəˋtɑgrəfɚ〕
攝影師

movie director
〔ˋmuvɪ dəˋrɛktɚ〕
導演

movie star
〔ˋmuvɪ star〕
電影明星

surveyor
〔səˋveɚ〕
測量技師

pianist
〔pɪ'ænɪst〕
鋼琴師

musician
〔mju'zɪʃən〕
音樂家

poet
〔'po·ɪt〕
詩人

illustrator
〔'ɪləs,tretɚ〕
插畫家

writer
〔'raɪtɚ〕
作家

cartoonist
〔kɑr'tunɪst〕
漫畫家

painter
〔'pentɚ〕
畫家

singer
〔'sɪŋɚ〕
歌手

baseball player
〔'bes'bɔl 'pleɚ〕
棒球選手

football player
〔'fʊt,bɔl 'pleɚ〕
橄欖球選手

soccer player
〔'sɑkɚ 'pleɚ〕
足球選手

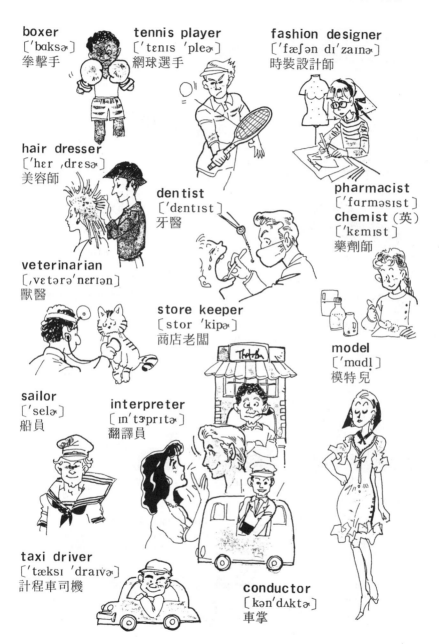

boxer
〔′bɑksə〕
拳擊手

tennis player
〔′tɛnɪs ′pleə〕
網球選手

fashion designer
〔′fæʃən dɪ′zaɪnə〕
時裝設計師

hair dresser
〔′hɛr ˌdrɛsə〕
美容師

dentist
〔′dɛntɪst〕
牙醫

pharmacist
〔′fɑrməsɪst〕
chemist (英)
〔′kɛmɪst〕
藥劑師

veterinarian
〔ˌvɛtərə′nɛrɪən〕
獸醫

store keeper
〔stor ′kipə〕
商店老闆

model
〔′mɑdl〕
模特兒

sailor
〔′selə〕
船員

interpreter
〔ɪn′tɝprɪtə〕
翻譯員

taxi driver
〔′tæksɪ ′draɪvə〕
計程車司機

conductor
〔kən′dʌktə〕
車掌

㊽交通　*Traffic*

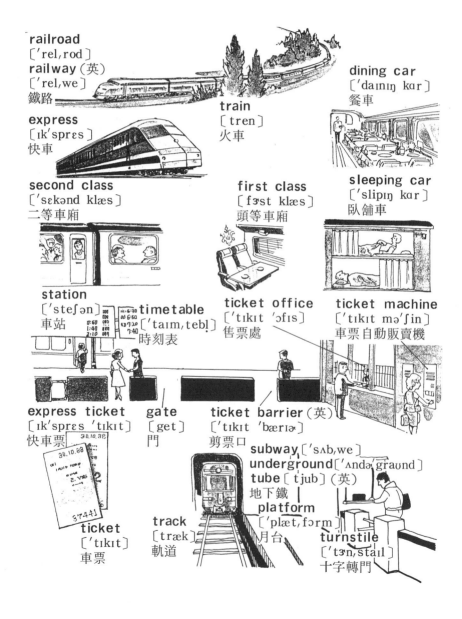

railroad
〔'rel,rod〕
railway（英）
〔'rel,we〕
鐵路

express
〔ɪk'sprɛs〕
快車

train
〔tren〕
火車

dining car
〔'daɪnɪŋ kɑr〕
餐車

second class
〔'sɛkənd klæs〕
二等車廂

first class
〔fɝst klæs〕
頭等車廂

sleeping car
〔'slipɪŋ kɑr〕
臥舖車

station
〔'steʃən〕
車站

timetable
〔'taɪm,tebl〕
時刻表

ticket office
〔'tɪkɪt 'ɔfɪs〕
售票處

ticket machine
〔'tɪkɪt mə'ʃin〕
車票自動販賣機

express ticket
〔ɪk'sprɛs 'tɪkɪt〕
快車票

gate
〔get〕
門

ticket barrier（英）
〔'tɪkɪt 'bæriɚ〕
剪票口

subway,〔'sʌb,we〕
underground〔'ʌndɚ'graʊnd〕
tube〔tjub〕（英）
地下鐵

platform
〔'plæt,fɔrm〕
月台

ticket
〔'tɪkɪt〕
車票

track
〔træk〕
軌道

turnstile
〔'tɝn,staɪl〕
十字轉門

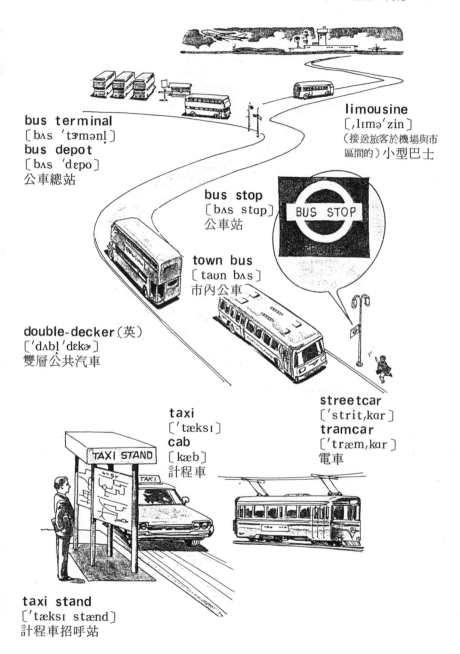

bus terminal
〔bʌs ˈtɝmənl〕
bus depot
〔bʌs ˈdɛpo〕
公車總站

limousine
〔ˌlɪməˈzin〕
（接送旅客於機場與市
區間的）小型巴士

bus stop
〔bʌs stɑp〕
公車站

BUS STOP

town bus
〔taʊn bʌs〕
市內公車

double-decker（英）
〔ˈdʌbl ˈdɛkɚ〕
雙層公共汽車

streetcar
〔ˈstrit,kɑr〕
tramcar
〔ˈtræm,kɑr〕
電車

taxi
〔ˈtæksɪ〕
cab
〔kæb〕
計程車

TAXI STAND

taxi stand
〔ˈtæksɪ stænd〕
計程車招呼站

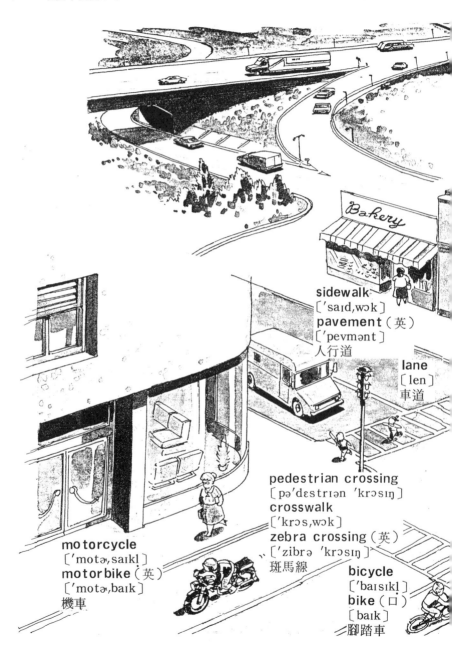

sidewalk
〔'saɪd,wɔk〕
pavement（英）
〔'pevmənt〕
人行道

lane
〔len〕
車道

pedestrian crossing
〔pə'dɛstrɪən 'krɔsɪŋ〕
crosswalk
〔'krɔs,wɔk〕
zebra crossing（英）
〔'zibrə 'krɔsɪŋ〕
斑馬線

motorcycle
〔'motɚ,saɪkl〕
motorbike（英）
〔'motɚ,baɪk〕
機車

bicycle
〔'baɪsɪkl〕
bike（口）
〔baɪk〕
脚踏車

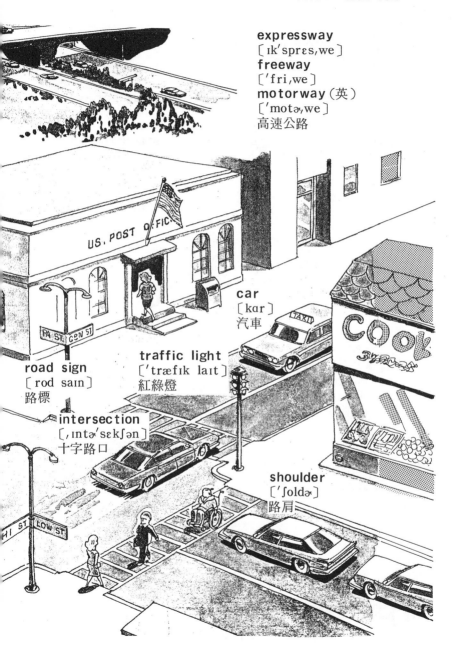

expressway
〔ɪkˈsprɛsˌwe〕
freeway
〔ˈfriˌwe〕
motorway (英)
〔ˈmotəˌwe〕
高速公路

car
〔kɑr〕
汽車

traffic light
〔ˈtræfɪk laɪt〕
紅綠燈

road sign
〔rod saɪn〕
路標

intersection
〔ˌɪntəˈsɛkʃən〕
十字路口

shoulder
〔ˈʃoldə〕
路肩

US. POST OFFIC

COOK

㊿ 汽車　*Automobile*

full-size car
〔ˈfʊl ˈsaɪz kɑr〕
大型車

passenger car
〔ˈpæsn̩dʒɚ kɑr〕
客車
standard-size car
〔ˈstændəd ˈsaɪz kɑr〕
中型車

compact-size car
〔ˈkɑmpækt ˈsaɪz kɑr〕
小型車

coupe
〔kup〕
雙門雙座小汽車

hardtop
〔ˈhɑrd.tɑp〕
鋼板車頂跑車

hatchback
〔ˈhætʃ.bæk〕
掀背式汽車

convertible
〔kənˈvɝtəbl̩〕
敞蓬車

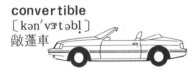

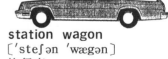

station wagon
〔ˈsteʃən ˈwægən〕
旅行車

pickup truck
〔ˈpɪk.ʌp trʌk〕
敞蓬運貨小卡車

truck
〔trʌk〕
貨車;卡車

van
〔væn〕
有蓋貨車

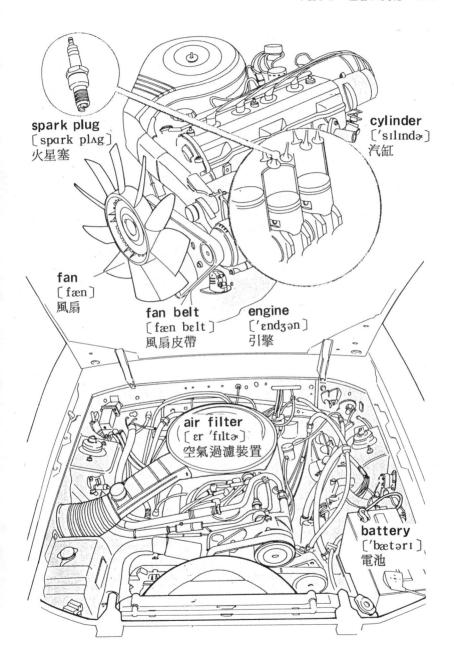

spark plug
〔spɑrk plʌg〕
火星塞

cylinder
〔'sɪlɪndɚ〕
汽缸

fan
〔fæn〕
風扇

fan belt
〔fæn bɛlt〕
風扇皮帶

engine
〔'ɛndʒən〕
引擎

air filter
〔ɛr 'fɪltɚ〕
空氣過濾裝置

battery
〔'bætərɪ〕
電池

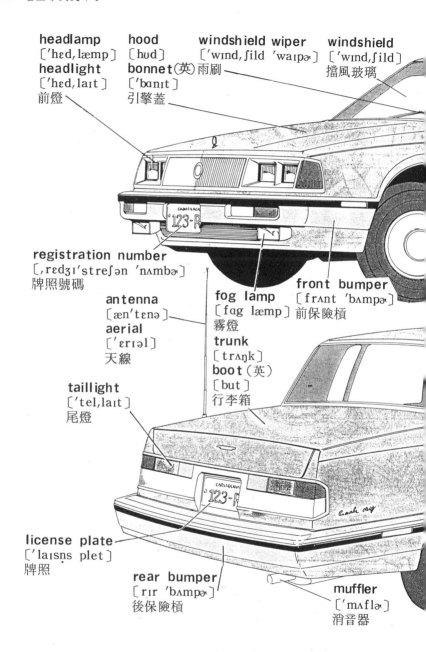

headlamp
〔'hɛd,læmp〕
headlight
〔'hɛd,laɪt〕
前燈

hood
〔hʊd〕
bonnet(英)
〔'banɪt〕
引擎蓋

windshield wiper
〔'wɪnd,ʃild 'waɪpɚ〕
雨刷

windshield
〔'wɪnd,ʃild〕
擋風玻璃

registration number
〔,rɛdʒɪ'streʃən 'nʌmbɚ〕
牌照號碼

antenna
〔æn'tɛnə〕
aerial
〔'ɛrɪəl〕
天線

fog lamp
〔fag læmp〕
霧燈

front bumper
〔frʌnt 'bʌmpɚ〕
前保險槓

trunk
〔trʌŋk〕
boot(英)
〔but〕
行李箱

taillight
〔'tel,laɪt〕
尾燈

license plate
〔'laɪsns plet〕
牌照

rear bumper
〔rɪr 'bʌmpɚ〕
後保險槓

muffler
〔'mʌflɚ〕
消音器

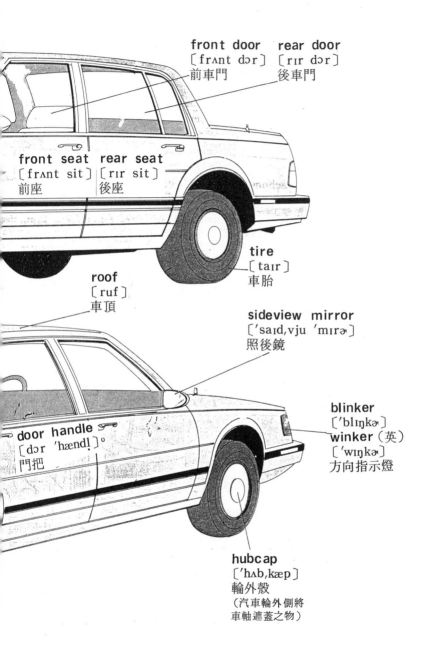

front door　rear door
〔frʌnt dɔr〕〔rɪr dɔr〕
前車門　　後車門

front seat　rear seat
〔frʌnt sit〕〔rɪr sit〕
前座　　　後座

tire
〔taɪr〕
車胎

roof
〔ruf〕
車頂

sideview mirror
〔'saɪd,vju 'mɪrɚ〕
照後鏡

blinker
〔'blɪŋkɚ〕
winker（英）
〔'wɪŋkɚ〕
方向指示燈

door handle
〔dɔr 'hændl〕
門把

hubcap
〔'hʌb,kæp〕
輪外殼
（汽車輪外側將
車軸遮蓋之物）

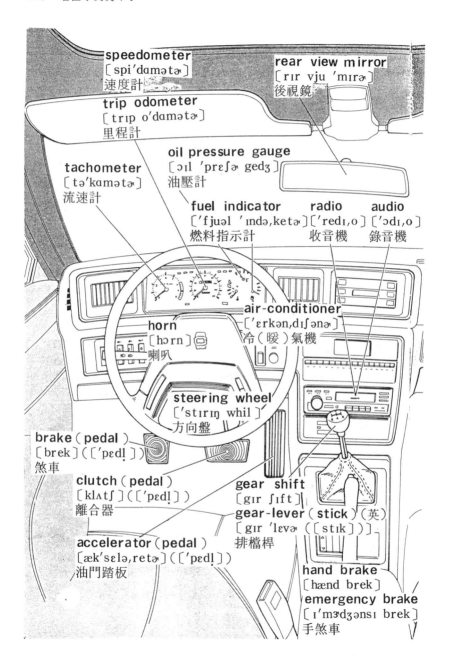

speedometer
〔spi'dɑmətɚ〕
速度計

rear view mirror
〔rɪr vju 'mɪrɚ〕
後視鏡

trip odometer
〔trɪp o'dɑmətɚ〕
里程計

oil pressure gauge
〔ɔɪl 'prɛʃɚ gedʒ〕
油壓計

tachometer
〔tə'kɑmətɚ〕
流速計

fuel indicator　**radio**　**audio**
〔'fjuəl 'ɪndə,ketɚ〕〔'redɪ,o〕〔'ɔdɪ,o〕
燃料指示計　　收音機　　錄音機

air-conditioner
〔'ɛrkən,dɪʃənɚ〕
冷（暖）氣機

horn
〔hɔrn〕
喇叭

steering wheel
〔'stɪrɪŋ whil〕
方向盤

brake（**pedal**）
〔brek〕（〔'pɛdl̩〕）
煞車

clutch（**pedal**）
〔klʌtʃ〕（〔'pɛdl̩〕）
離合器

gear shift
〔gɪr ʃɪft〕

gear-lever（**stick**）（英）
〔gɪr 'lɛvɚ（〔stɪk〕））
排檔桿

accelerator（**pedal**）
〔æk'sɛlə,retɚ〕（〔'pɛdl̩〕）
油門踏板

hand brake
〔hænd brek〕

emergency brake
〔ɪ'mɝdʒənsɪ brek〕
手煞車

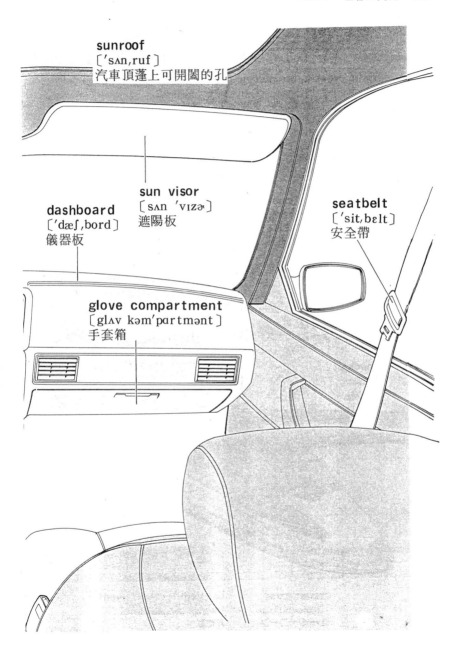

sunroof
〔'sʌn͵ruf〕
汽車頂蓬上可開闊的孔

sun visor
〔sʌn 'vɪzɚ〕
遮陽板

dashboard
〔'dæʃ͵bord〕
儀器板

seatbelt
〔'sit͵bɛlt〕
安全帶

glove compartment
〔glʌv kəm'pɑrtmənt〕
手套箱

⑤飛機及機場 *Airplane and Airport*

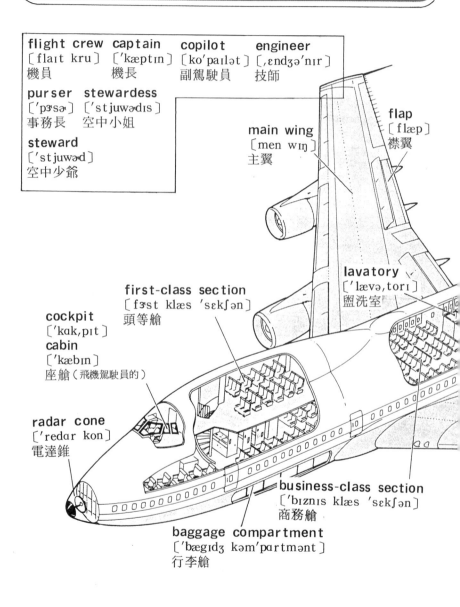

flight crew captain
〔flaɪt kru〕 〔'kæptɪn〕
機員   機長

copilot   engineer
〔ko'paɪlət〕 〔,ɛndʒə'nɪr〕
副駕駛員   技師

purser stewardess
〔'pɝsɚ〕 〔'stjuwədɪs〕
事務長   空中小姐

steward
〔'stjuwəd〕
空中少爺

main wing
〔men wɪŋ〕
主翼

flap
〔flæp〕
襟翼

lavatory
〔'lævə,torɪ〕
盥洗室

first-class section
〔fɝst klæs 'sɛkʃən〕
頭等艙

cockpit
〔'kɑk,pɪt〕
cabin
〔'kæbɪn〕
座艙(飛機駕駛員的)

radar cone
〔'redɑr kon〕
雷達錐

business-class section
〔'bɪznɪs klæs 'sɛkʃən〕
商務艙

baggage compartment
〔'bægɪdʒ kəm'pɑrtmənt〕
行李艙

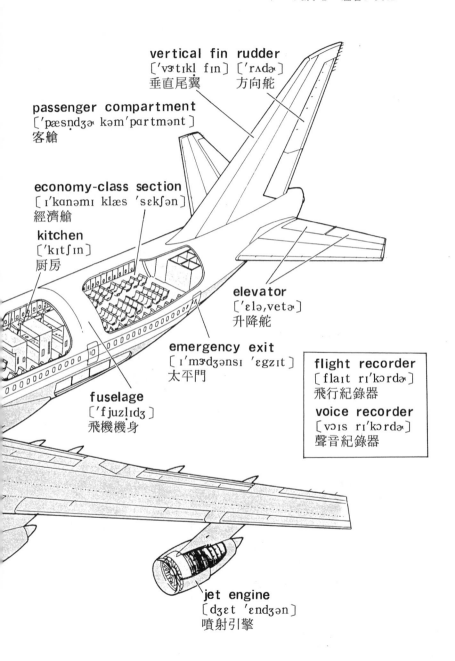

vertical fin　**rudder**
〔'vɜ˞tɪkl fɪn〕〔'rʌdə˞〕
垂直尾翼　　方向舵

passenger compartment
〔'pæsndʒə˞ kəm'pɑrtmənt〕
客艙

economy-class section
〔ɪ'kɑnəmɪ klæs 'sɛkʃən〕
經濟艙

kitchen
〔'kɪtʃɪn〕
厨房

elevator
〔'ɛlə,vetə˞〕
升降舵

emergency exit
〔ɪ'mɜ˞dʒənsɪ 'ɛgzɪt〕
太平門

flight recorder
〔flaɪt rɪ'kɔrdə˞〕
飛行紀錄器

voice recorder
〔vɔɪs rɪ'kɔrdə˞〕
聲音紀錄器

fuselage
〔'fjuzlɪdʒ〕
飛機機身

jet engine
〔dʒɛt 'ɛndʒən〕
噴射引擎

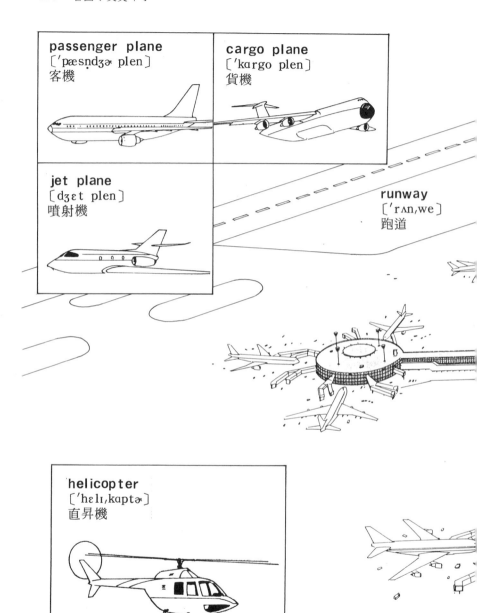

passenger plane
〔'pæsṇdʒɚ plen〕
客機

cargo plane
〔'kɑrgo plen〕
貨機

jet plane
〔dʒɛt plen〕
噴射機

runway
〔'rʌn,we〕
跑道

helicopter
〔'hɛlɪ,kɑptɚ〕
直昇機

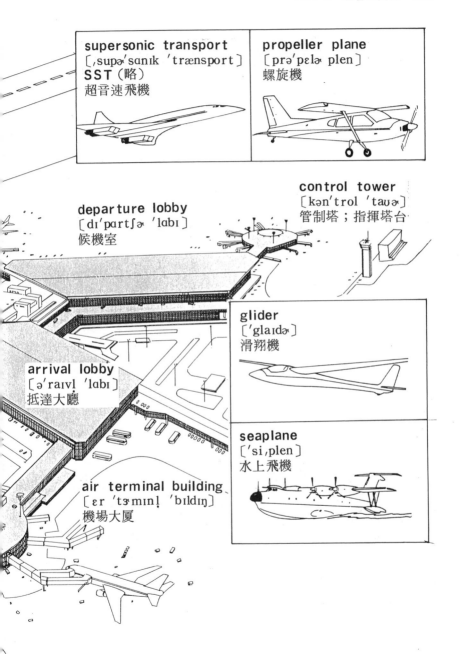

supersonic transport
〔,supə'sɑnɪk 'trænsport〕
SST (略)
超音速飛機

propeller plane
〔prə'pɛlə plen〕
螺旋機

control tower
〔kən'trol 'tauə〕
管制塔；指揮塔台

departure lobby
〔dɪ'pɑrtʃə 'lɑbɪ〕
候機室

glider
〔'glaɪdə〕
滑翔機

arrival lobby
〔ə'raɪvl 'lɑbɪ〕
抵達大廳

seaplane
〔'si,plen〕
水上飛機

air terminal building
〔ɛr 'tɜmɪnḷ 'bɪldɪŋ〕
機場大廈

㊾ 船　　*Ship*

rowboat
〔'ro,bot〕
划艇

yacht
〔jɑt〕
遊艇

sailboat
〔'sel,bot〕
帆船

cruiser
〔'kruzɚ〕
巡洋艦

motorboat/powerboat
〔'motɚ,bot〕/〔'pauɚ,bot〕
汽艇

cargo boat
〔'kɑrgo bot〕
貨船

freighter
〔'fretɚ〕
貨輪

container ship
〔kən'tenɚ ʃɪp〕
貨櫃船

automobile carrier
〔'ɔtəmə,bɪl 'kærɪɚ〕
汽車搬運船

ore carrier
〔or 'kærɪɚ〕
礦石搬運船

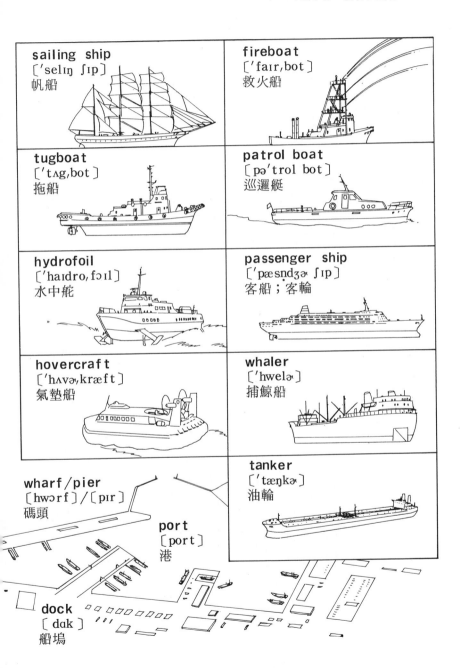

sailing ship
〔'selɪŋ ʃɪp〕
帆船

fireboat
〔'faɪr,bot〕
救火船

tugboat
〔'tʌg,bot〕
拖船

patrol boat
〔pə'trol bot〕
巡邏艇

hydrofoil
〔'haɪdro,fɔɪl〕
水中舵

passenger ship
〔'pæsndʒɚ ʃɪp〕
客船；客輪

hovercraft
〔'hʌvɚ,kræft〕
氣墊船

whaler
〔'hwelɚ〕
捕鯨船

tanker
〔'tæŋkɚ〕
油輪

wharf/pier
〔hwɔrf〕/〔pɪr〕
碼頭

port
〔port〕
港

dock
〔dɑk〕
船塢

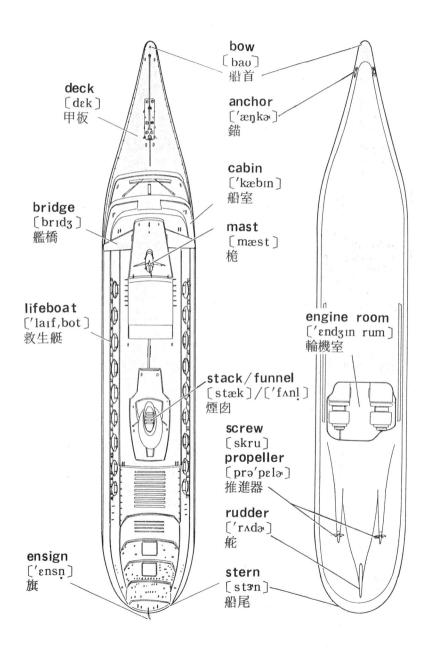

bow
〔baʊ〕
船首

deck
〔dɛk〕
甲板

anchor
〔'æŋkɚ〕
錨

cabin
〔'kæbɪn〕
船室

bridge
〔brɪdʒ〕
艦橋

mast
〔mæst〕
桅

lifeboat
〔'laɪf,bot〕
救生艇

engine room
〔'ɛndʒɪn rum〕
輪機室

stack / funnel
〔stæk〕/〔'fʌnl̩〕
煙囪

screw
〔skru〕
propeller
〔prə'pɛlɚ〕
推進器

rudder
〔'rʌdɚ〕
舵

ensign
〔'ɛnsn̩〕
旗

stern
〔stɝn〕
船尾

㊝美術 *Art*

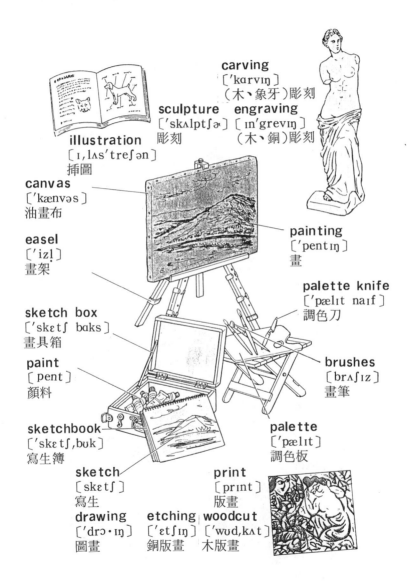

carving
〔'kɑrvɪŋ〕
（木、象牙）彫刻

sculpture
〔'skʌlptʃɚ〕
彫刻

engraving
〔ɪn'grevɪŋ〕
（木、銅）彫刻

illustration
〔ɪ,lʌs'treʃən〕
插圖

canvas
〔'kænvəs〕
油畫布

easel
〔'izl〕
畫架

painting
〔'pentɪŋ〕
畫

palette knife
〔'pælɪt naɪf〕
調色刀

sketch box
〔'skɛtʃ bɑks〕
畫具箱

paint
〔pent〕
顏料

brushes
〔brʌʃɪz〕
畫筆

sketchbook
〔'skɛtʃ,bʊk〕
寫生簿

palette
〔'pælɪt〕
調色板

sketch
〔skɛtʃ〕
寫生

print
〔prɪnt〕
版畫

drawing
〔'drɔ·ɪŋ〕
圖畫

etching
〔'ɛtʃɪŋ〕
銅版畫

woodcut
〔'wʊd,kʌt〕
木版畫

(54) 音樂 *Music*

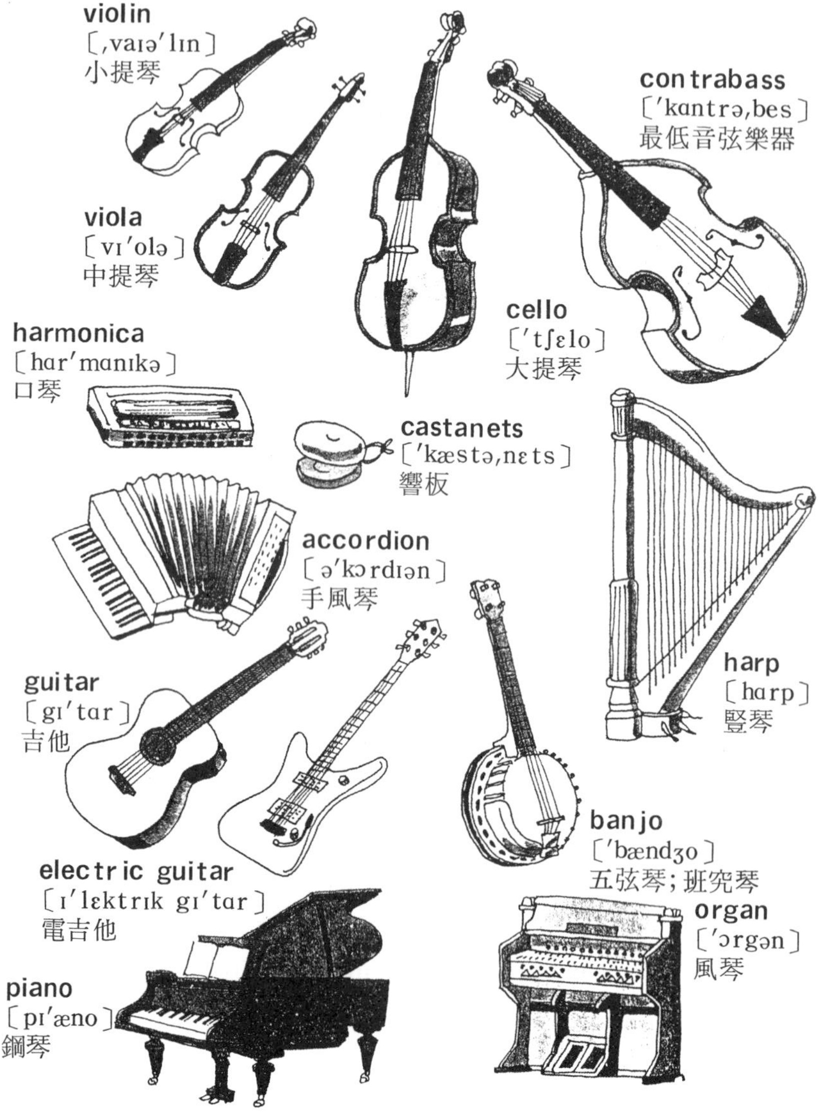
violin
〔ˌvaɪəˈlɪn〕
小提琴
viola
〔vɪˈolə〕
中提琴
contrabass
〔ˈkɑntrəˌbes〕
最低音弦樂器
cello
〔ˈtʃɛlo〕
大提琴
harmonica
〔hɑrˈmɑnɪkə〕
口琴
castanets
〔ˈkæstəˌnɛts〕
響板
accordion
〔əˈkɔrdɪən〕
手風琴
harp
〔hɑrp〕
豎琴
guitar
〔gɪˈtɑr〕
吉他
banjo
〔ˈbændʒo〕
五弦琴；班究琴
electric guitar
〔ɪˈlɛktrɪk gɪˈtɑr〕
電吉他
organ
〔ˈɔrgən〕
風琴
piano
〔pɪˈæno〕
鋼琴

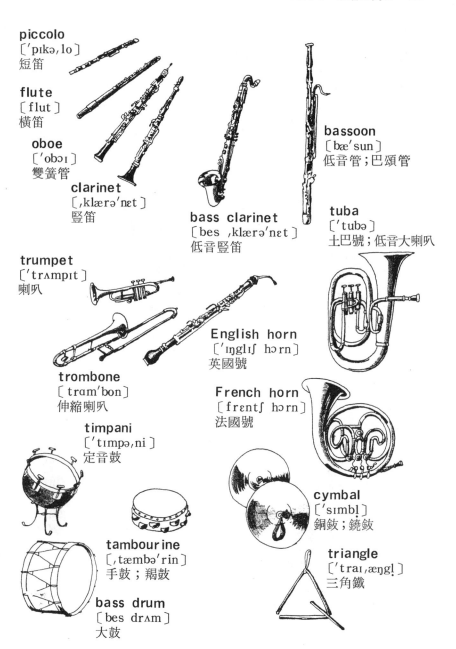

piccolo
〔ˈpɪkəˌlo〕
短笛

flute
〔flut〕
橫笛

oboe
〔ˈobɔɪ〕
雙簧管

clarinet
〔ˌklærəˈnɛt〕
豎笛

bass clarinet
〔bes ˌklærəˈnɛt〕
低音豎笛

bassoon
〔bæˈsun〕
低音管；巴頌管

tuba
〔ˈtubə〕
土巴號；低音大喇叭

trumpet
〔ˈtrʌmpɪt〕
喇叭

English horn
〔ˈɪŋglɪʃ hɔrn〕
英國號

trombone
〔trɑmˈbon〕
伸縮喇叭

French horn
〔frɛntʃ hɔrn〕
法國號

timpani
〔ˈtɪmpəˌni〕
定音鼓

cymbal
〔ˈsɪmbl〕
銅鈸；鐃鈸

tambourine
〔ˌtæmbəˈrin〕
手鼓；羯鼓

triangle
〔ˈtraɪˌæŋgl〕
三角鐵

bass drum
〔bes drʌm〕
大鼓

55 戲劇　　　*Play*

classical play
〔'klæsɪkl ple〕
古典戲劇

avant-garde play
〔ɑvã 'gɑrd ple〕
前衛戲劇

opera
〔'ɑpərə〕
歌劇

opera singer
〔'ɑpərə 'sɪŋə〕
歌劇演唱家

musical
〔'mjuzɪkl〕
歌舞劇

curtain
〔'kɝtɪn〕
窗帘

gallery
〔'gælərɪ〕
頂層樓座
（票價最低廉）

lines
〔laɪnz〕
台詞

actress
〔'æktrɪs〕
女演員

auditorium
〔͵ɔdə'torɪəm〕
聽衆席

actor
〔'æktɚ〕
演員

script
〔skrɪpt〕
劇本

director
〔də'rɛktɚ〕
導演

playwright
〔'ple͵raɪt〕

dramatist
〔'dræmətɪst〕
劇作家

stage
〔stedʒ〕
舞台

performance
〔pɚ'fɔrməns〕
演出

㊏ 文化資產 *Cultural Assets*

garden
〔'gɑrdn̩〕
花園

art museum
〔ɑrt mju'ziəm〕
gallery
〔'gælərɪ〕
美術館

castle
〔'kæsl̩〕
城堡

museum
〔mju'ziəm〕
博物館

palace
〔'pælɪs〕
宮殿

opera house
〔'ɑpərə haʊs〕
歌劇院

church/cathedral
〔tʃɝtʃ〕/〔kə'θidrəl〕
教會／大教堂

music hall
〔'mjuzɪk hɔl〕
音樂廳

ruins
〔'ruɪnz〕
遺跡

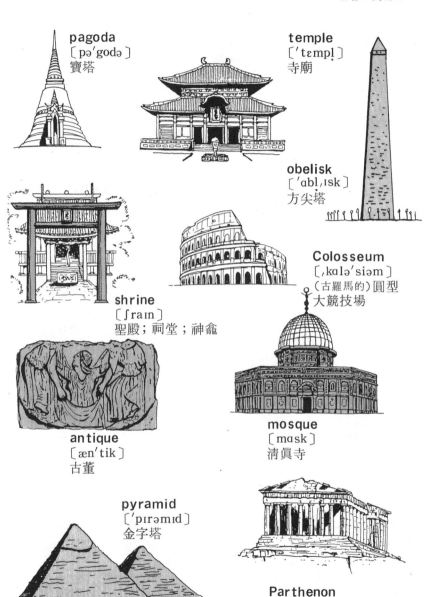

pagoda
〔pə'godə〕
寶塔

temple
〔'tɛmpl̩〕
寺廟

obelisk
〔'abl̩,ısk〕
方尖塔

shrine
〔ʃraın〕
聖殿；祠堂；神龕

Colosseum
〔,kɑlə'sıəm〕
（古羅馬的）圓型
大競技場

antique
〔æn'tik〕
古董

mosque
〔mɑsk〕
清眞寺

pyramid
〔'pırəmıd〕
金字塔

Parthenon
〔'pɑrθə,nɑn〕
巴特農神殿
（在希臘雅典的 Athena 女神神殿）

㊗️ 運動　　　*Sports*

the Olympic Games
〔ðɪ oˈlɪmpɪk gemz〕
奧林匹克運動會

Summer Olympics
〔ˈsʌmɚ oˈlɪmpɪks〕
夏季奧林匹克運動會

track
〔træk〕
徑賽

field
〔fild〕
田賽

gymnastics
〔dʒɪmˈnæstɪks〕
體操

swimming
〔ˈswɪmɪŋ〕
游泳

volleyball
〔ˈvɑlɪˌbɔl〕
排球

badminton
〔ˈbædmɪntən〕
羽球

soccer
〔ˈsɑkɚ〕
足球

judo
〔ˈdʒudo〕
柔道

equestrian
〔ɪˈkwɛstrɪən〕
騎術家

table tennis
〔ˈtebḷ ˈtɛnɪs〕
桌球

wrestling
〔′rɛsəlɪŋ〕
摔角

fencing
〔′fɛnsɪŋ〕
西洋劍

handball
〔′hænd,bɔl〕
手球

hockey
〔′hɑkɪ〕
曲棍球

weight lifting
〔wet ′lɪftɪŋ〕
舉重

cycling
〔′saɪklɪŋ〕
自行車

archery
〔′ɑrtʃərɪ〕
射箭

canoeing
〔kə′nuɪŋ〕
泛舟

shooting
〔′ʃutɪŋ〕
射擊

rowing
〔′roɪŋ〕
划船

yachting
〔′jɑtɪŋ〕
駕遊艇

tennis
〔′tɛnɪs〕
網球

Winter Olympics
〔ˈwɪntɚ oˈlɪmpɪks〕
冬季奧林匹克運動會

ski jump
〔ski dʒʌmp〕
滑雪跳

Alpine sking
〔ˈælpaɪn skɪŋ〕
高山滑雪

figure skating
〔ˈfɪgɚ ˈsketɪŋ〕
花式溜冰

speed skating
〔ˈspid ˈsketɪŋ〕
快速溜冰

ice hockey
〔aɪs ˈhɑkɪ〕
冰上曲棍球

bobsled
〔ˈbɑbslɛd〕
連橇

luge
〔luʒ〕
競賽用的
小型雪橇

biathlon
〔ˈbaɪæθlən〕
二十公里四點
射聲滑雪賽

football
〔'fʊt,bɔl〕
足球（英）
橄欖球（美）

baseball
〔'bes'bɔl〕
棒球

rugby
〔'rʌgbɪ〕
橄欖球

karate
〔ka'rɑte〕
空手道

golf
〔gɑlf〕
高爾夫球

dancing
〔'dænsɪŋ〕
跳舞

mountain climbing
〔'maʊntn̩ 'klaɪmɪŋ〕
登山

bowling
〔'bolɪŋ〕
保齡球

softball
〔'sɔft,bɔl〕
壘球

squash
〔skwɑʃ〕
回力球

⑱休閒活動 *Leisure*

gambling
['gæmblɪŋ]
賭博

roulette
[ru'lɛt]
輪盤賭

TV game (=*video gam*
[ti vi gem]
電視遊樂器

slot machine
[slɑt mə'ʃin]
吃角子老虎

casino
[kə'sino]
賭場

darts
〔dɑrts〕
擲飛鏢

domino
〔'dɑmə,no〕
骨牌遊戲

chess
〔tʃɛs〕
西洋棋

backgammon
〔,bæk'gæmən〕
西洋雙陸棋

blackjack
〔'blæk,dʒæk〕
二十一點

cards
〔kɑrdz〕
撲克牌

billiards
〔'bɪljədz〕

pool
〔pul〕
撞球

skydiving
〔'skaɪ,daɪvɪŋ〕
(在打開降落傘以前用種種姿
勢操縱身體的)跳傘運動

hang gliding
〔hæŋ 'glaɪdɪŋ〕
懸動式滑翔機

frisbee
〔'frɪzbɪ〕
飛盤

roller skating
〔'rolɚ sketɪŋ〕
輪鞋溜冰

skateboard
〔'sket,bɔrd〕
滑板

windsurfing
〔'wɪnd,sɝfɪŋ〕
衝浪(衝浪板上有桅杆
和帆,利用風力行進)

surfing
〔'sɝfɪŋ〕
衝浪

surfboard
〔'sɝf,bord〕
衝浪板

skin diving
〔skɪn 'daɪvɪŋ〕
切膚潛水(僅備水肺及脚上鰭狀橡皮肢,而不穿潛水衣)

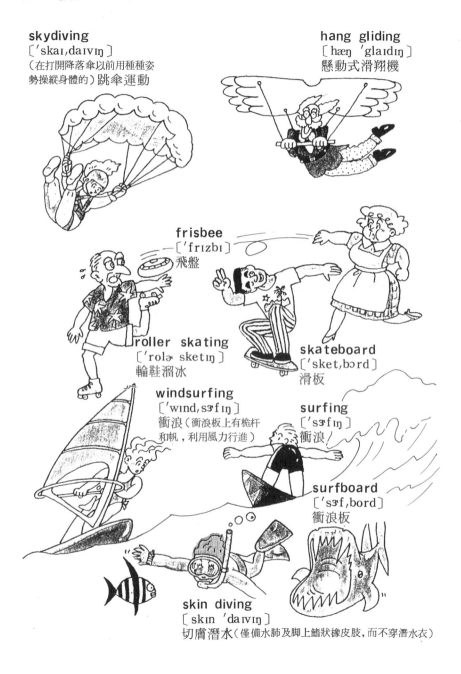

car race
〔kɑr res〕
賽車

horseback riding
〔'hɔrs,bæk 'raɪdɪŋ〕
騎馬

rodeo
〔'rodi,o〕
牛仔絕技競演會

horse racing
〔hɔrs 'resɪŋ〕
賽馬

hunting
〔'hʌntɪŋ〕
打獵

camp
〔kæmp〕
露營

picnic
〔'pɪknɪk〕
野餐

fishing
〔'fɪʃɪŋ〕
釣魚

(59) 節日及行事 *Holidays and Events*

New Year's Day
〔nju jɪrz de〕
元旦（1月1日）

St. Valentine's Day
〔sent ˈvæləntaɪnz de〕
情人節（2月14日）

Easter
〔ˈistɚ〕
復活節（3月下旬～4月上旬）

Independence Day
〔ˌɪndɪˈpɛndəns de〕
獨立紀念日（7月4日）

Christmas
〔ˈkrɪsməs〕
聖誕節（12月25日）

Halloween
〔ˌhælo'in〕
All Saint's Day
〔ɔl sents de〕
萬聖節

Thanksgiving Day
〔ˌθæŋksˈgɪvɪŋ de〕
感恩節（11月最後一個星期四）

⑥照相機 *Camera*

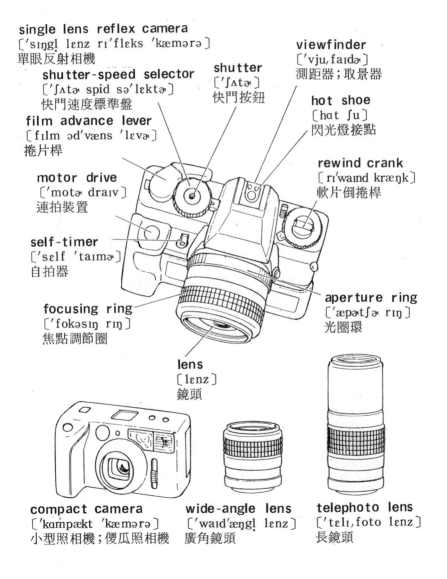

single lens reflex camera
〔'sɪŋl lɛnz rɪ'flɛks 'kæmərə〕
單眼反射相機

shutter-speed selector
〔'ʃʌtɚ spid sə'lɛktɚ〕
快門速度標準盤

film advance lever
〔fɪlm əd'væns 'lɛvɚ〕
捲片桿

motor drive
〔'motɚ draɪv〕
連拍裝置

self-timer
〔'sɛlf 'taɪmɚ〕
自拍器

focusing ring
〔'fokəsɪŋ rɪŋ〕
焦點調節圈

shutter
〔'ʃʌtɚ〕
快門按鈕

viewfinder
〔'vju,faɪdɚ〕
測距器；取景器

hot shoe
〔hɑt ʃu〕
閃光燈接點

rewind crank
〔rɪ'waɪnd kræŋk〕
軟片倒捲桿

aperture ring
〔'æpɚtʃɚ rɪŋ〕
光圈環

lens
〔lɛnz〕
鏡頭

compact camera
〔'kɑmpækt 'kæmərə〕
小型照相機；傻瓜照相機

wide-angle lens
〔'waɪd'æŋgl lɛnz〕
廣角鏡頭

telephoto lens
〔'tɛlɪ,foto lɛnz〕
長鏡頭

flashlight
［'flæʃ, laɪt］
閃光燈

exposure meter
［ɪk'spoʒɚ 'mitɚ］
曝光表

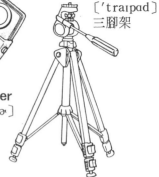

tripod
［'traɪpɑd］
三腳架

black and white film
［'blækən 'hwaɪt fɪlm］
黑白底片

negative color film
［'nɛɡətɪv 'kʌlɚ fɪlm］
彩色負片

reversal color film
［rɪ'vɝsəl 'kʌlɚ fɪlm］
彩色正片

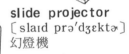

slide projector
［slaɪd prə'dʒɛktɚ］
幻燈機

slide
［slaɪd］
幻燈片

video recorder
［'vɪdɪ,o rɪ'kɔrdɚ］
電視錄放影機

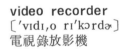

video camera
［'vɪdɪ,o 'kæmərə］
錄影機

⑥ 音響 *Audio*

audio set
〔ˈɔdɪ,o ,sɛt〕
音響

turntable
〔ˈtɝn,tebḷ〕
轉盤

player
〔ˈpleɚ〕
唱盤

CD player
〔si di ˈpleɚ〕
雷射唱盤

tuner
〔ˈtjunɚ〕
調音器

amplifier
〔ˈæmplə,faɪɚ〕
擴音器

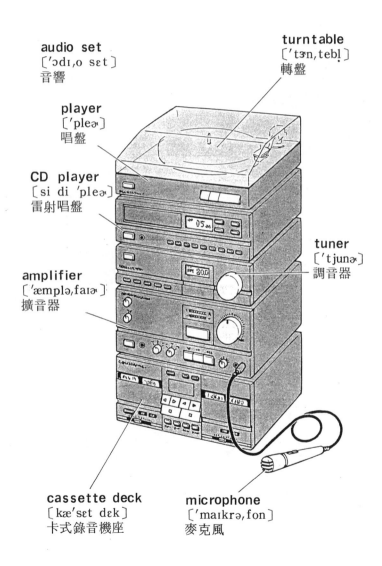

cassette deck
〔kæˈsɛt dɛk〕
卡式錄音機座

microphone
〔ˈmaɪkrə,fon〕
麥克風

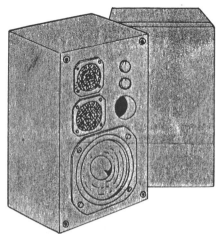

speaker
〔'spikɚ〕
擴音喇叭

cassette tape
〔kæ'sɛt tep〕
錄音帶

compact disk
〔'kɑmpækt dɪsk〕
雷射唱盤

record/disk
〔'rɛkəd〕/〔dɪsk〕
唱片

headphones
〔'hɛd,fonz〕
耳機

radio-cassette tape recorder
〔'redɪ,o kæ'sɛt tep rɪ'kɔrdɚ〕
收錄音機

Part 3

生 物

LIFE

(62) 微生物及菌類 *Microbes and Fungi*

mold
〔mold〕
霉

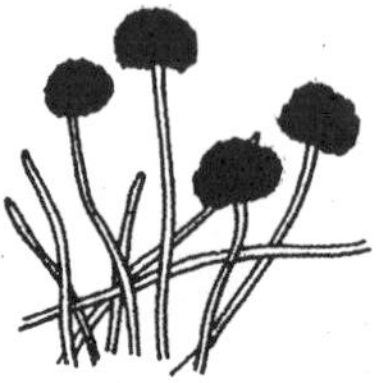

toadstool
〔'tod,stul〕
菌(特指毒菌)

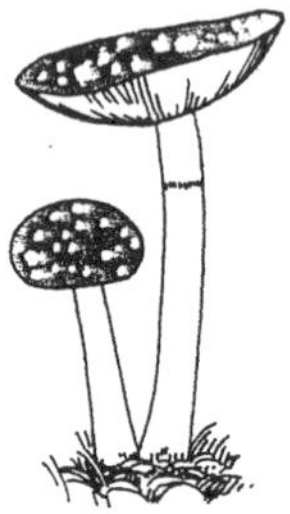

paramecium
〔ˌpærə'miʃɪəm〕
草履蟲

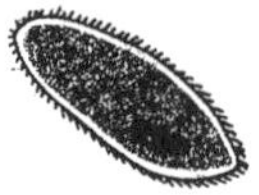

amoeba
〔ə'mibə〕
阿米巴;變形蟲

mushroom
〔'mʌʃrʊm〕
蕈

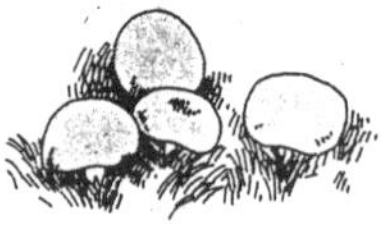

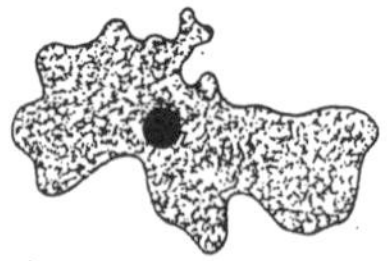

lactic bacilli
〔'læktɪk bə'sɪlaɪ〕
乳酸菌

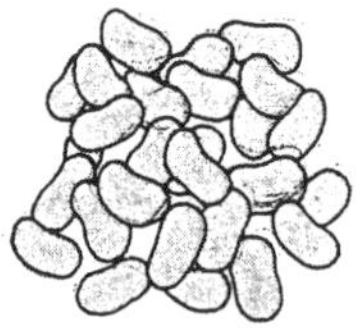

colon bacilli
〔'kolən bə'sɪlaɪ〕
大腸菌

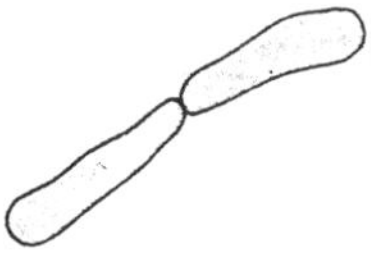

plankton
〔'plæŋktən〕
浮游生物

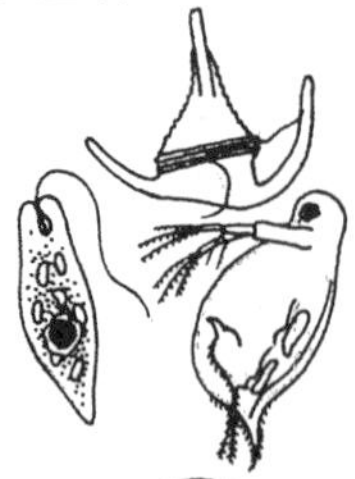

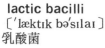

dropper
〔'drɑpɚ〕
滴管

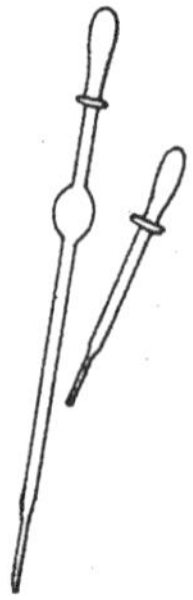

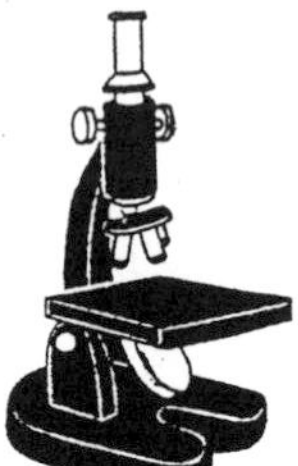

microscope
〔'maɪkrə,skop〕
顯微鏡

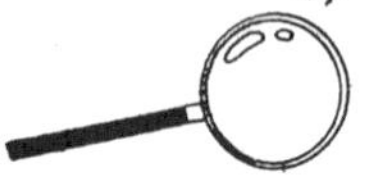

magnifying glass
〔'mægnə,faɪɪŋ glæs〕
放大鏡

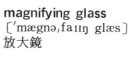

⑥植物各部分名稱　*Parts of a Plant*

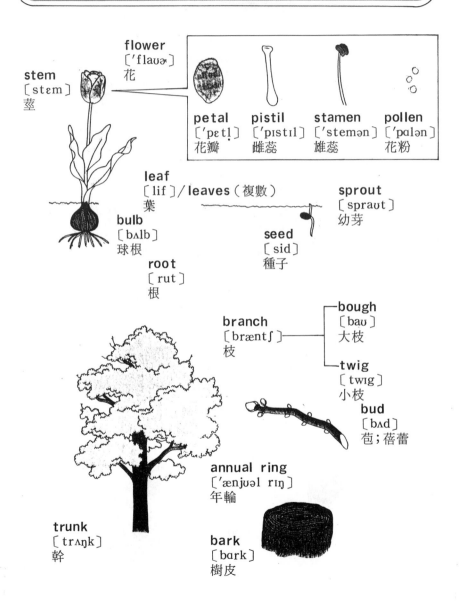

stem
〔stεm〕
莖

flower
〔'flauɚ〕
花

petal
〔'pεt!〕
花瓣

pistil
〔'pɪstɪl〕
雌蕊

stamen
〔'stemən〕
雄蕊

pollen
〔'palən〕
花粉

leaf
〔lif〕/**leaves**（複數）
葉

bulb
〔bʌlb〕
球根

root
〔rut〕
根

seed
〔sid〕
種子

sprout
〔spraut〕
幼芽

branch
〔bræntʃ〕
枝

bough
〔bau〕
大枝

twig
〔twɪg〕
小枝

bud
〔bʌd〕
苞；蓓蕾

annual ring
〔'ænjuəl rɪŋ〕
年輪

trunk
〔trʌŋk〕
幹

bark
〔bark〕
樹皮

 ㉔ 花   *Flowers*

cherry blossom
〔'tʃɛrɪ 'blɑsəm〕
櫻花

sunflower
〔'sʌn,flauɚ〕
向日葵

cosmos
〔'kɑzməs〕
大波斯菊；美
洲可思莫思花

sweet pea
〔swit pi〕
香豌豆(的花)

crocus
〔'krokəs〕
蕃紅花

chrysanthemum
〔krɪs'ænθəməm〕
菊

iris
〔'aɪrɪs〕
鳶尾花

pansy
〔'pænzɪ〕
三色紫羅蘭

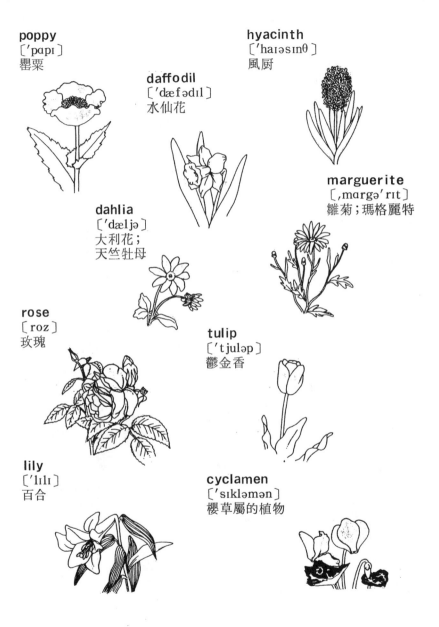

poppy
〔'pɑpɪ〕
罌粟

hyacinth
〔'haɪəsɪnθ〕
風厨

daffodil
〔'dæfədɪl〕
水仙花

marguerite
〔,mɑrgə'rɪt〕
雛菊；瑪格麗特

dahlia
〔'dæljə〕
大利花；
天竺牡母

rose
〔roz〕
玫瑰

tulip
〔'tjuləp〕
鬱金香

lily
〔'lɪlɪ〕
百合

cyclamen
〔'sɪkləmən〕
櫻草屬的植物

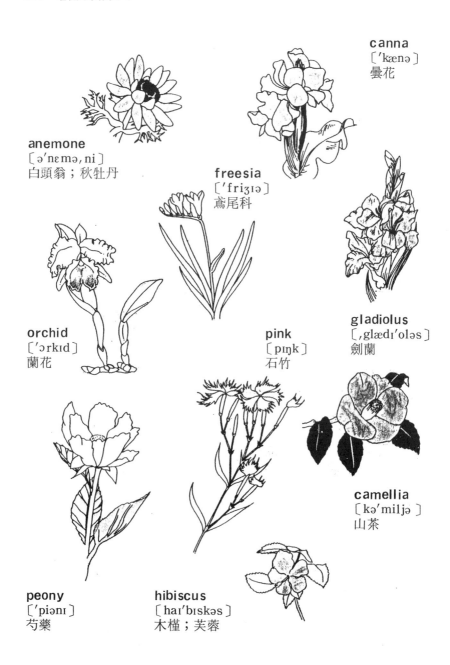

canna
〔'kænə〕
曇花

anemone
〔ə'nɛmə,ni〕
白頭翁；秋牡丹

freesia
〔'friʒɪə〕
鳶尾科

gladiolus
〔,glædɪ'oləs〕
劍蘭

orchid
〔'ɔrkɪd〕
蘭花

pink
〔pɪŋk〕
石竹

camellia
〔kə'miljə〕
山茶

peony
〔'piənɪ〕
芍藥

hibiscus
〔haɪ'bɪskəs〕
木槿；芙蓉

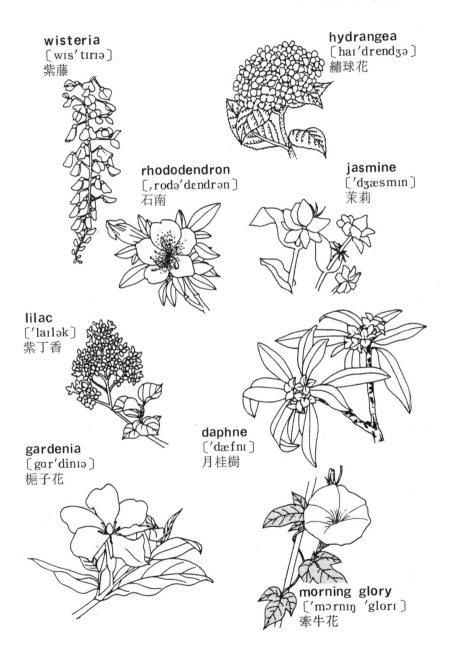

wisteria
〔wɪs'tɪrɪə〕
紫藤

hydrangea
〔haɪ'drɛndʒə〕
繡球花

rhododendron
〔͵rodə'dɛndrən〕
石南

jasmine
〔'dʒæsmɪn〕
茉莉

lilac
〔'laɪlək〕
紫丁香

gardenia
〔gɑr'dinɪə〕
梔子花

daphne
〔'dæfnɪ〕
月桂樹

morning glory
〔'mɔrnɪŋ 'glorɪ〕
牽牛花

㊳ 野草、水草及其他 *Wild Grass, Water plants and Others*

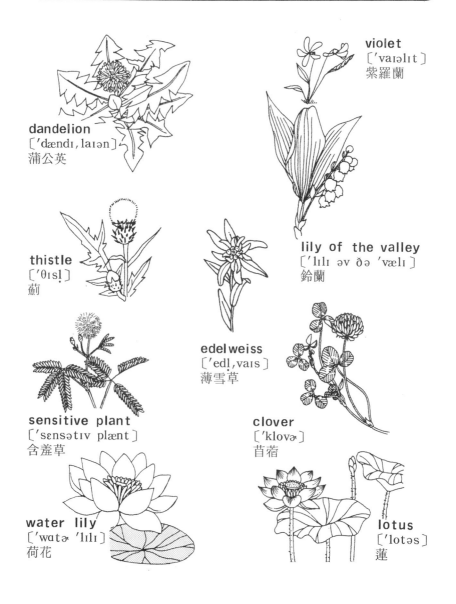

dandelion
〔'dændɪ,laɪən〕
蒲公英

violet
〔'vaɪəlɪt〕
紫羅蘭

thistle
〔'θɪsl〕
薊

lily of the valley
〔'lɪlɪ əv ðə 'vælɪ〕
鈴蘭

edelweiss
〔'edl,vaɪs〕
薄雪草

sensitive plant
〔'sɛnsətɪv plænt〕
含羞草

clover
〔'klovɚ〕
苜蓿

water lily
〔'wɑtɚ 'lɪlɪ〕
荷花

lotus
〔'lotəs〕
蓮

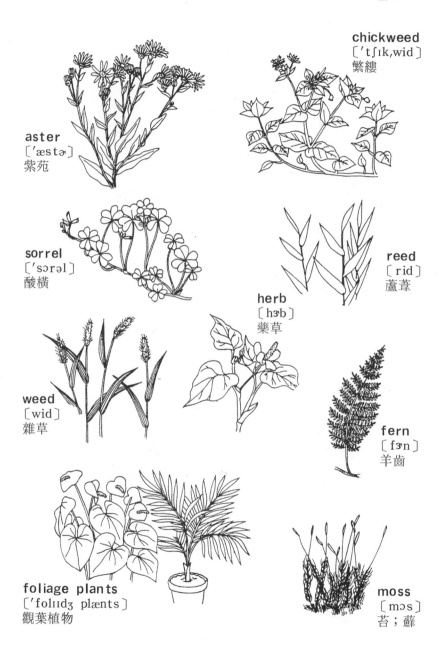

chickweed
〔'tʃɪk,wid〕
繁縷

aster
〔'æstɚ〕
紫苑

sorrel
〔'sɔrəl〕
酸橫

reed
〔rid〕
蘆葦

herb
〔hɝb〕
藥草

weed
〔wid〕
雜草

fern
〔fɝn〕
羊齒

foliage plants
〔'folɪɪdʒ plænts〕
觀葉植物

moss
〔mɔs〕
苔；蘚

⑥ 樹　　　*Trees*

broadleaf tree
〔'brɔd,lif tri〕
濶葉樹

camphor tree
〔'kæmfɚ tri〕
樟樹

eucalyptus
〔,jukə'lɪptəs〕
由加利樹

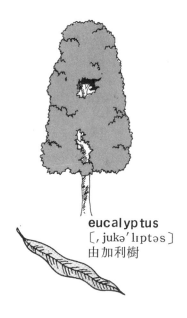

wattle
〔'wɑtl〕
金合歡的一種

box
〔bɑks〕
黃楊木

conifer
〔'kɔnəfɚ〕
針葉樹

sequoia
〔sɪ'kwɔɪə〕
水杉

pine
〔paɪn〕
松樹

cedar
〔'sidɚ〕
西洋杉

Japanese cedar
〔,dʒæpə'niz 'sidɚ〕
日本杉

fir
〔fɝ〕
樅樹

cypress
〔'saɪprəs〕
柏樹

deciduous tree
〔dɪˈsɪdʒʊəs tri〕
落葉樹

oak
〔ok〕
橡樹

poplar
〔ˈpɑplɚ〕
白楊

ginkgo
〔ˈdʒɪŋko〕
銀杏
（＝*gingko*）

elm
〔ɛlm〕
榆樹

maple
〔ˈmepḷ〕
槭

larch
〔lɑrtʃ〕
落葉松

horse chestnut
〔hɔrs ˈtʃɛs,nʌt〕
七葉樹

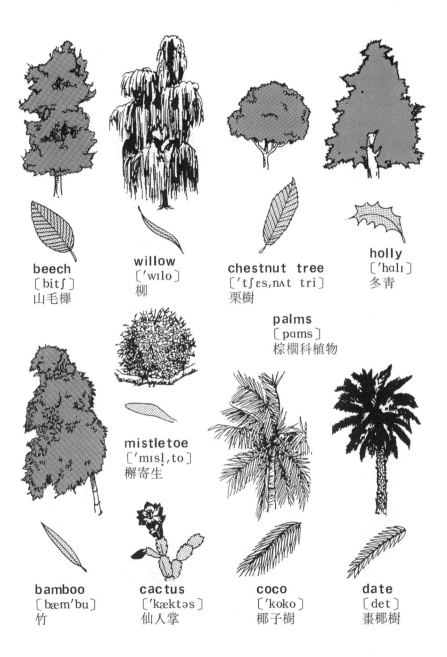

beech
〔bitʃ〕
山毛欅

willow
〔'wɪlo〕
柳

chestnut tree
〔'tʃɛs,nʌt tri〕
栗樹

holly
〔'hɑlɪ〕
冬青

palms
〔pɑms〕
棕櫚科植物

mistletoe
〔'mɪsl̩,to〕
檞寄生

bamboo
〔bæm'bu〕
竹

cactus
〔'kæktəs〕
仙人掌

coco
〔'koko〕
椰子樹

date
〔det〕
棗椰樹

⑥ 動物　*Animals*

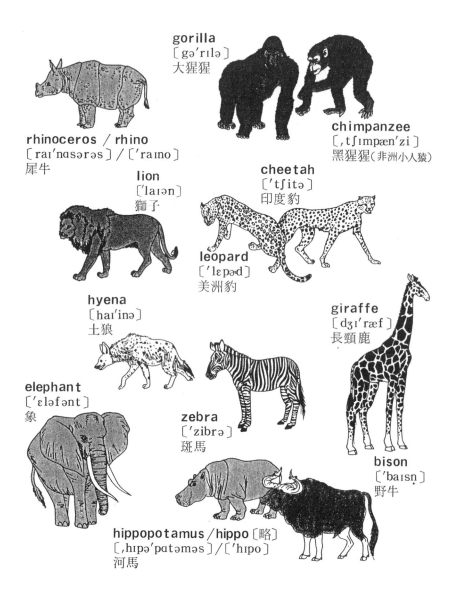

gorilla
〔gəˋrɪlə〕
大猩猩

chimpanzee
〔͵tʃɪmpænˋzi〕
黑猩猩(非洲小人猿)

rhinoceros / rhino
〔raɪˋnɑsərəs〕/〔ˋraɪno〕
犀牛

lion
〔ˋlaɪən〕
獅子

cheetah
〔ˋtʃitə〕
印度豹

leopard
〔ˋlɛpəd〕
美洲豹

hyena
〔haɪˋinə〕
土狼

giraffe
〔dʒɪˋræf〕
長頸鹿

elephant
〔ˋɛləfənt〕
象

zebra
〔ˋzibrə〕
斑馬

bison
〔ˋbaɪsn〕
野牛

hippopotamus /hippo〔略〕
〔͵hɪpəˋpɑtəməs〕/〔ˋhɪpo〕
河馬

puma
〔'pjumə〕
美洲獅

deer
〔dɪr〕
鹿

bear
〔bɛr〕
熊

wildcat
〔'waɪld,kæt〕
山貓

wolf
〔wʊlf〕
狼

raccoon
〔ræ'kun〕
浣熊

jackal
〔'dʒækɔl〕
狐狼

fox
〔fɑks〕
狐

raccoon dog
〔ræ'kun dɔg〕
狸

reindeer
〔'ren,dɪr〕
馴鹿

beaver
〔'bivɚ〕
海狸

polar bear
〔'polɚ bɛr〕
北極熊

orangutan
〔oˊræŋʊˌtæn〕
猩猩（婆羅洲與蘇門答臘巨猿，在林間食果實樹葉）

giant panda
〔ˊdʒaɪənt ˊpændə〕
貓熊

yak
〔jæk〕
犛牛

monkey
〔ˊmʌŋkɪ〕
猴

camel
〔ˊkæml〕
駱駝

koala bear
〔kəˊɑlə bɛr〕
無尾熊

kangaroo
〔ˌkæŋɡəˊru〕
袋鼠

hare
〔hɛr〕
野兔

rabbit
〔ˊræbɪt〕
兔子

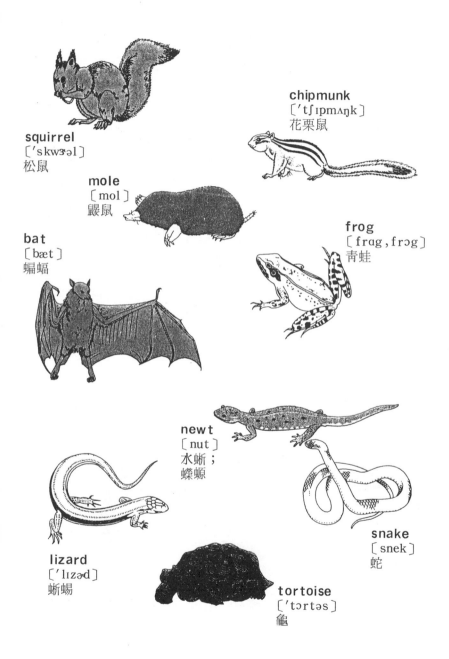

squirrel
〔'skwɜ˞əl〕
松鼠

chipmunk
〔'tʃɪpmʌŋk〕
花栗鼠

mole
〔mol〕
鼴鼠

bat
〔bæt〕
蝙蝠

frog
〔frɑg, frɔg〕
青蛙

newt
〔nut〕
水蜥；
蠑螈

lizard
〔'lɪzəd〕
蜥蜴

snake
〔snek〕
蛇

tortoise
〔'tɔrtəs〕
龜

⑱鳥　　　　　*Birds*

parakeet
〔'pærə,kit〕
小鸚鵡

canary
〔kə'nɛrɪ〕
金絲雀

sparrow
〔'spæro〕
麻雀

swallow
〔'swɑlo〕
燕子

parrot
〔'pærət〕
鸚鵡

duck
〔dʌk〕
野鴨

goose
〔gus〕
鵝

swan
〔swɑn〕
天鵝

heron
〔'hɛrən〕
蒼鷺

woodpecker
〔'wʊd,pɛkɚ〕
啄木鳥

hawk
〔hɔk〕
鷹

eagle
〔'igl〕
鷹

falcon
〔'fɔlkən〕
獵鷹

crow
〔kro〕
烏鴉

jay
〔dʒe〕
樫鳥

kingfisher
〔'kɪŋ,fɪʃɚ〕
翠鳥

pigeon
〔'pɪdʒɪn〕
鴿子

peacock
〔'pi,kɑk〕
孔雀

robin
〔'rɑbɪn〕
知更鳥

sea gull
〔si gʌl〕
海鷗

thrush
〔θrʌʃ〕
畫眉

owl
〔aʊl〕
貓頭鷹

horned owl
〔'hɔrnɪd aʊl〕
鴟鵂

skylark
〔'skaɪ,lark〕
雲雀

ostrich
〔'ɔstrɪtʃ〕
鴕鳥

nightingale
〔'naɪtɪŋ,gel〕
夜鶯

blackbird
〔'blæk,bɝd〕
山鳥

cardinal
〔'kardənl〕
紅雀；紅冠鳥

㊲寵物及家禽 *Pets and Domestic Animals*

horse
〔hɔrs〕
馬

donkey
〔'dɑŋkɪ〕
驢子

foal
〔fol〕
（馬、驢等
的）仔，小馬

cow
〔kaʊ〕
母牛；乳牛

calf
〔kæf〕
小牛

pony
〔'ponɪ〕
小馬

piglet
〔'pɪglɪt〕
小豬

turkey
〔't͟ɝkɪ〕
火雞

pig
〔pɪg〕
豬

sheep
〔ʃip〕
綿羊

lamb
〔læm〕
小羊

goat
〔got〕
山羊

chick
〔tʃɪk〕
小雞

hen
〔hɛn〕
母雞

rooster
〔'rustɚ〕
雄雞

kid
〔kɪd〕
小山羊

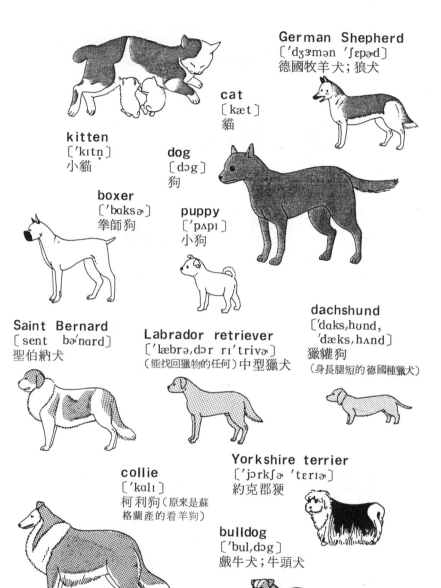

German Shepherd
〔'dʒɝmən 'ʃɛpəd〕
德國牧羊犬；狼犬

cat
〔kæt〕
貓

kitten
〔'kɪtn̩〕
小貓

dog
〔dɔg〕
狗

boxer
〔'bɑksɚ〕
拳師狗

puppy
〔'pʌpɪ〕
小狗

dachshund
〔'dɑks,hʊnd,
 'dæks,hʌnd〕
獵貛狗
（身長腿短的德國種獵犬）

Saint Bernard
〔sent bɚ'nɑrd〕
聖伯納犬

Labrador retriever
〔'læbrə,dɔr rɪ'trivɚ〕
（能找回獵物的任何）中型獵犬

collie
〔'kɑlɪ〕
柯利狗（原來是蘇
格蘭產的看羊狗）

Yorkshire terrier
〔'jɔrkʃɚ 'tɛrɪə〕
約克郡㹴

bulldog
〔'bul,dɔg〕
戲牛犬；牛頭犬

⑦ 昆蟲及蟲　　　*Insects and Worms*

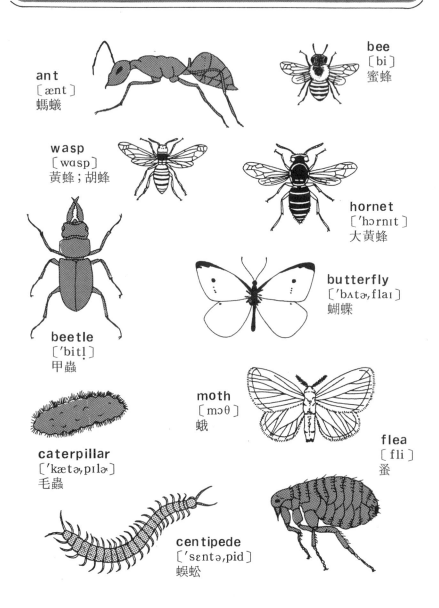

ant
〔ænt〕
螞蟻

bee
〔bi〕
蜜蜂

wasp
〔wɑsp〕
黃蜂；胡蜂

hornet
〔ˈhɔrnɪt〕
大黃蜂

beetle
〔ˈbitl̩〕
甲蟲

butterfly
〔ˈbʌtɚˌflaɪ〕
蝴蝶

moth
〔mɔθ〕
蛾

flea
〔fli〕
蚤

caterpillar
〔ˈkætɚˌpɪlɚ〕
毛蟲

centipede
〔ˈsɛntəˌpid〕
蜈蚣

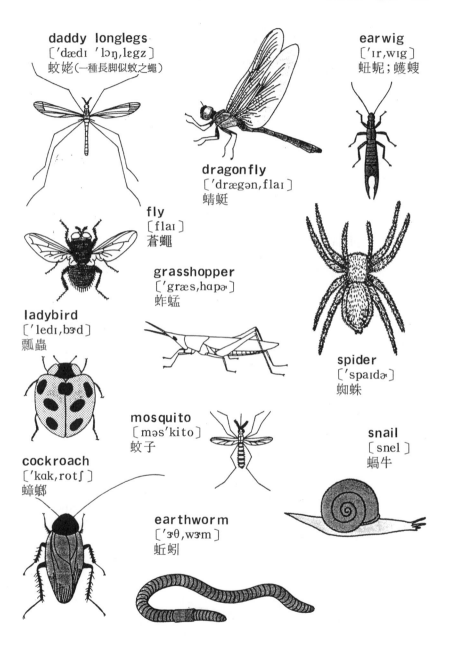

daddy longlegs
〔'dædɪ 'lɔŋ,lɛgz〕
蚊姥(一種長脚似蚊之蠅)

earwig
〔'ɪr,wɪg〕
蚰蜒；蠼螋

dragonfly
〔'drægən,flaɪ〕
蜻蜓

fly
〔flaɪ〕
蒼蠅

grasshopper
〔'græs,hɑpɚ〕
蚱蜢

ladybird
〔'ledɪ,bɝd〕
瓢蟲

spider
〔'spaɪdɚ〕
蜘蛛

mosquito
〔məs'kito〕
蚊子

snail
〔snel〕
蝸牛

cockroach
〔'kɑk,rotʃ〕
蟑螂

earthworm
〔'ɝθ,wɝm〕
蚯蚓

㉒魚 *Fishes*

goldfish
〔'gold'fɪʃ〕
金魚

angelfish
〔'endʒl,fɪʃ〕
神仙魚

seahorse
〔'si,hɔrs〕
海馬

piranha
〔pɪ'rɑnjə〕
南美產的食人魚
（貪食，在水中會襲擊人獸）

carp
〔kɑrp〕
鯉魚

guppy
〔'gʌpɪ〕
古比（產於西印
度群島熱帶魚）

crucian carp
〔'kruʃən kɑrp〕
鯽魚

catfish
〔'kæt,fɪʃ〕
鯰魚

loach
〔lotʃ〕
泥鰍

rainbow trout
〔'ren,bo traʊt〕
虹鱒魚

eel
〔il〕
鰻魚

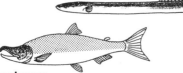 

sardine
〔sɑr'din〕
沙丁魚

salmon
〔'sæmən〕
鮭魚

herring
〔'hɛrɪŋ〕
鯡魚

tuna
〔'tunə〕
鮪魚

swordfish
〔'sord,fıʃ〕
旗魚

mackerel
〔'mækrəl〕
鯖

cod
〔kɑd〕
鱈魚
（＝*codfish*）

sea bream
〔si brim〕
海鯛

bonito
〔bə'nito〕
松魚；鰹

flying fish
〔'flaııŋ fıʃ〕
飛魚

halibut
〔'hæləbət〕
大比目魚

turbot
〔'tɝbət〕
比目魚之類

globefish
〔'glob,fıʃ〕
河豚

ray
〔re〕
魟魚

sunfish
〔'sʌn,fıʃ〕
翻車魚

shark
〔ʃɑrk〕
鯊魚

saury pike
〔'sɔrı paık〕
秋刀魚

⑦ 海洋生物　*Marine Life*

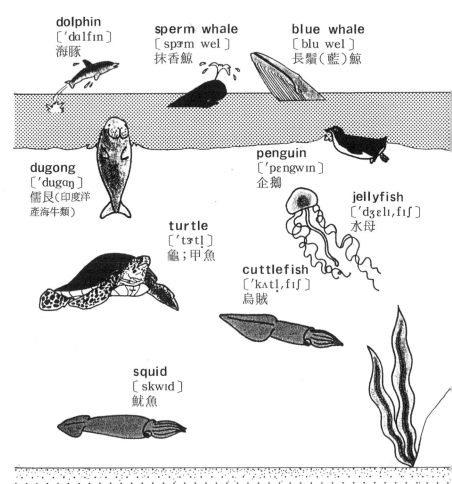

dolphin
〔ˈdɑlfɪn〕
海豚

sperm whale
〔spɝm wel〕
抹香鯨

blue whale
〔blu wel〕
長鬚（藍）鯨

dugong
〔ˈdugɑŋ〕
儒艮（印度洋
產海牛類）

penguin
〔ˈpɛngwɪn〕
企鵝

jellyfish
〔ˈdʒɛlɪˌfɪʃ〕
水母

turtle
〔ˈtɝtl̩〕
龜；甲魚

cuttlefish
〔ˈkʌtl̩ˌfɪʃ〕
烏賊

squid
〔skwɪd〕
魷魚

oyster
〔ˈɔɪstɚ〕
蠔；牡蠣

clam
〔klæm〕
蛤；蚌

top shell
〔tɑpˈʃɛl〕
外殼呈有規則圓
錐形的軟體動物

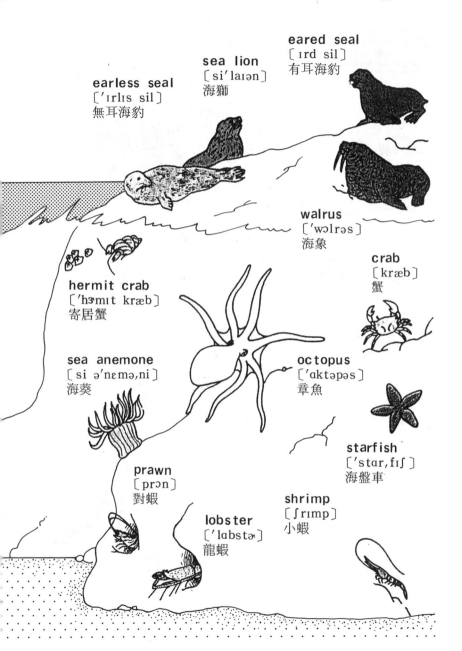

eared seal
〔ɪrd sil〕
有耳海豹

sea lion
〔si'laɪən〕
海獅

earless seal
〔'ɪrlɪs sil〕
無耳海豹

walrus
〔'wɔlrəs〕
海象

crab
〔kræb〕
蟹

hermit crab
〔'hɜˈmɪt kræb〕
寄居蟹

sea anemone
〔si ə'nɛmə,ni〕
海葵

octopus
〔'ɑktəpəs〕
章魚

starfish
〔'star,fɪʃ〕
海盤車

prawn
〔prɔn〕
對蝦

shrimp
〔ʃrɪmp〕
小蝦

lobster
〔'labstɚ〕
龍蝦

(73) 動物的叫聲 *The Cries*

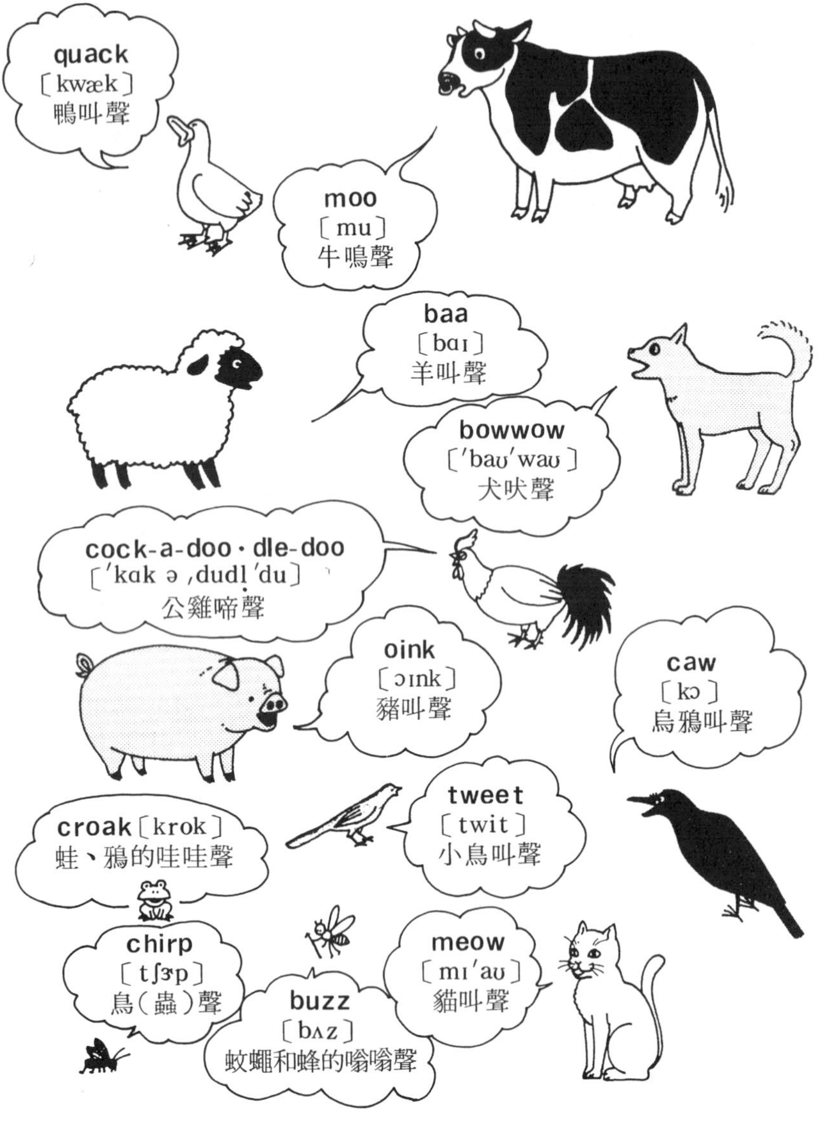

Part 4

宇宙及自然現象

SPACE AND NATURE

⑦宇宙 *Universe*

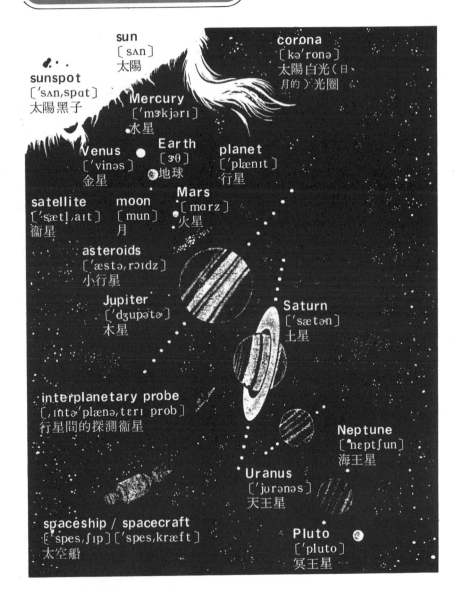

sun
〔sʌn〕
太陽

sunspot
〔'sʌn,spɑt〕
太陽黑子

corona
〔kə'ronə〕
太陽白光（日、
月的）光圈

Mercury
〔'mɝkjərɪ〕
水星

Venus
〔'vinəs〕
金星

Earth
〔ɝθ〕
地球

planet
〔'plænɪt〕
行星

satellite
〔'sætḷ,aɪt〕
衛星

moon
〔mun〕
月

Mars
〔mɑrz〕
火星

asteroids
〔'æstə,rɔɪdz〕
小行星

Jupiter
〔'dʒupətɚ〕
木星

Saturn
〔'sætɚn〕
土星

interplanetary probe
〔,ɪntɚ'plænə,tɛrɪ prob〕
行星間的探測衛星

Neptune
〔'nɛptʃun〕
海王星

Uranus
〔'jurənəs〕
天王星

spaceship / spacecraft
〔'spes,ʃɪp〕〔'spes,kræft〕
太空船

Pluto
〔'pluto〕
冥王星

galaxy.
〔'gæləksɪ〕
銀河

nebula
〔'nɛbjʊlə〕
星雲

black hole
〔blæk hol〕
黑洞

comet
〔'kɑmɪt〕
彗星

lunar rover
〔ˋlunɚ ˋrovɚ〕
月球車

lunar module
〔ˋlunɚ ˋmɑdʒul〕
登月小艇

space shuttle
〔spes ˋʃʌtl〕
太空梭

（man-made）satellite
〔（ˋmænˎmed）ˋsætlˎaɪt〕
人造衞星

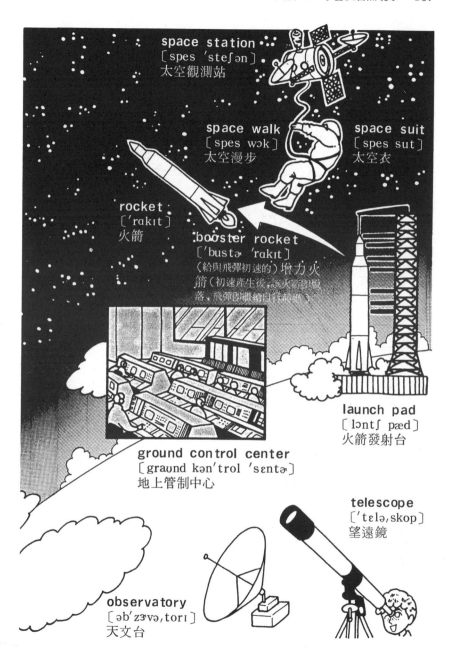

space station
〔spes 'steʃən〕
太空觀測站

space walk
〔spes wɔk〕
太空漫步

space suit
〔spes sut〕
太空衣

rocket
〔'rɑkɪt〕
火箭

booster rocket
〔'bustɚ 'rɑkɪt〕
(給與飛彈初速的)增力火
箭(初速產生後,該火箭即脫
落,飛彈即繼續自行前進)

launch pad
〔lɔntʃ pæd〕
火箭發射台

ground control center
〔graʊnd kən'trol 'sɛntɚ〕
地上管制中心

telescope
〔'tɛlə,skop〕
望遠鏡

observatory
〔əb'zɝvə,torɪ〕
天文台

⑦⑤星座 *Constellations*

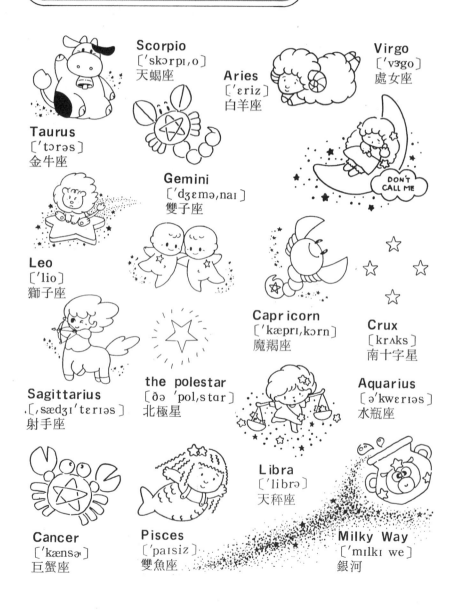

Scorpio
〔'skɔrpɪ͵o〕
天蝎座

Aries
〔'ɛriz〕
白羊座

Virgo
〔'vɜgo〕
處女座

Taurus
〔'tɔrəs〕
金牛座

Gemini
〔'dʒɛmə͵naɪ〕
雙子座

DON'T CALL ME

Leo
〔'lio〕
獅子座

Capricorn
〔'kæprɪ͵kɔrn〕
魔羯座

Crux
〔krʌks〕
南十字星

Sagittarius
〔͵sædʒɪ'tɛrɪəs〕
射手座

the polestar
〔ðə 'pol͵star〕
北極星

Aquarius
〔ə'kwɛrɪəs〕
水瓶座

Cancer
〔'kænsə〕
巨蟹座

Pisces
〔'paɪsiz〕
雙魚座

Libra
〔'librə〕
天秤座

Milky Way
〔'mɪlkɪ we〕
銀河

⑯ 地球　*Earth*

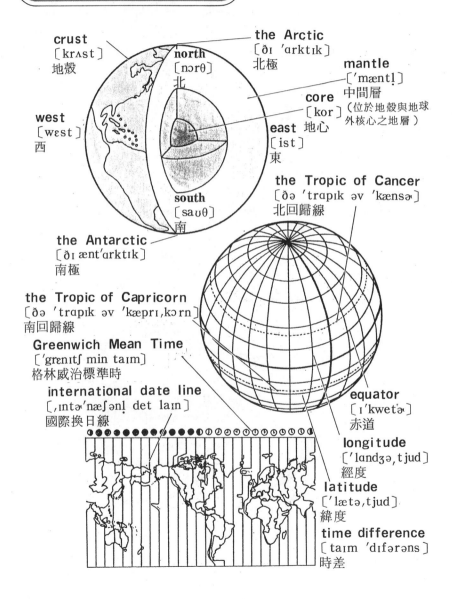

crust
〔krʌst〕
地殼

the Arctic
〔ðɪ ˈɑrktɪk〕
北極

mantle
〔ˈmæntl̩〕
中間層
（位於地殼與地球
外核心之地層）

north
〔nɔrθ〕
北

core
〔kor〕
地心

west
〔wɛst〕
西

east
〔ist〕
東

south
〔saʊθ〕
南

the Tropic of Cancer
〔ðə ˈtrɑpɪk əv ˈkænsə〕
北回歸線

the Antarctic
〔ðɪ ænt'ɑrktɪk〕
南極

the Tropic of Capricorn
〔ðə ˈtrɑpɪk əv ˈkæprɪˌkɔrn〕
南回歸線

Greenwich Mean Time
〔ˈgrɛnɪtʃ min taɪm〕
格林威治標準時

international date line
〔ˌɪntəˈnæʃənl̩ det laɪn〕
國際換日線

equator
〔ɪˈkwetə〕
赤道

longitude
〔ˈlɑndʒəˌtjud〕
經度

latitude
〔ˈlætəˌtjud〕
緯度

time difference
〔taɪm ˈdɪfərəns〕
時差

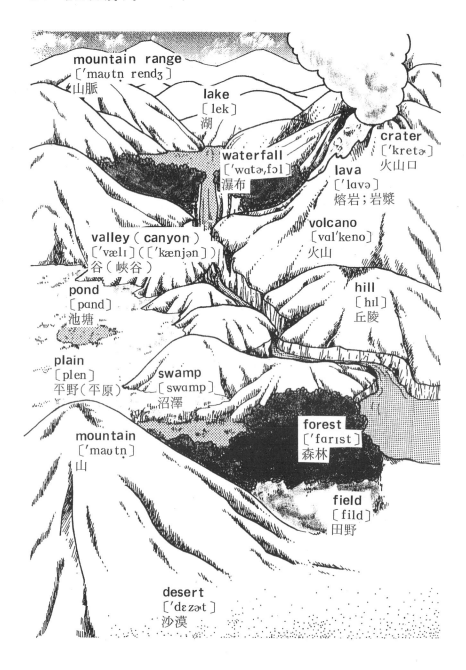

mountain range
〔ˈmaʊtn̩ rendʒ〕
山脈

lake
〔lek〕
湖

crater
〔ˈkretə〕
火山口

waterfall
〔ˈwatəˌfɔl〕
瀑布

lava
〔ˈlavə〕
熔岩；岩漿

valley（canyon）
〔ˈvælɪ〕（〔ˈkænjən〕）
谷（峽谷）

volcano
〔valˈkeno〕
火山

pond
〔pand〕
池塘

hill
〔hɪl〕
丘陵

plain
〔plen〕
平野（平原）

swamp
〔swamp〕
沼澤

forest
〔ˈfarɪst〕
森林

mountain
〔ˈmaʊtn̩〕
山

field
〔fild〕
田野

desert
〔ˈdɛzət〕
沙漠

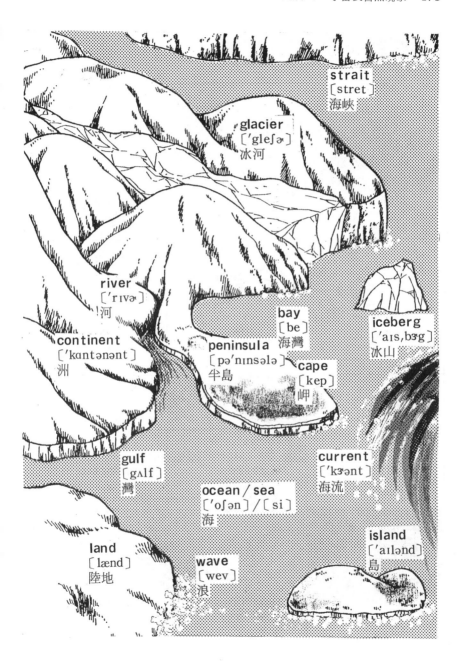

strait
〔stret〕
海峽

glacier
〔'gleʃɚ〕
冰河

river
〔'rɪvɚ〕
河

bay
〔be〕
海灣

peninsula
〔pə'nɪnsələ〕
半島

cape
〔kep〕
岬

iceberg
〔'aɪs,bɝg〕
冰山

continent
〔'kɑntənənt〕
洲

gulf
〔gʌlf〕
灣

current
〔'kɝənt〕
海流

ocean / sea
〔'oʃən〕/〔si〕
海

island
〔'aɪlənd〕
島

land
〔lænd〕
陸地

wave
〔wev〕
浪

⑦ 氣候　*Weather*

clear
〔klɪr〕
晴朗無雲的

fair
〔fɛr〕
晴朗的

cloudy
〔'klaʊdɪ〕
有雲的

rain
〔ren〕
雨

shower
〔'ʃaʊɚ〕
陣雨

fog
〔fɑg〕
霧

snow
〔sno〕
雪

snowstorm
〔'sno,stɔrm〕
blizzard
〔'blɪzəd〕
暴風雪

thunderstorm
〔'θʌndɚ,stɔrm〕
雷雨

lightning
〔'laɪtnɪŋ〕
閃電

typhoon
〔taɪ'fun〕
颱風

hurricane
〔'hɝɪ,ken〕
颶風；暴風

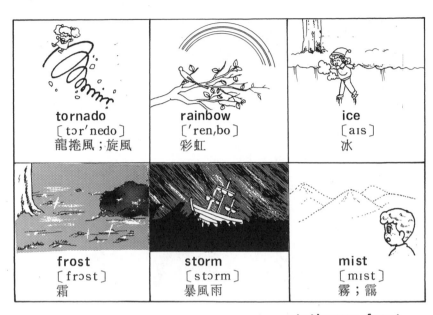

tornado
〔tɔrˊnedo〕
龍捲風；旋風

rainbow
〔ˊrenˌbo〕
彩虹

ice
〔aɪs〕
冰

frost
〔frɔst〕
霜

storm
〔stɔrm〕
暴風雨

mist
〔mɪst〕
霧；靄

warm front
〔wɔrm frʌnt〕
暖鋒

stationary front
〔ˊsteʃənˌɛrɪ frʌnt〕
滯流鋒

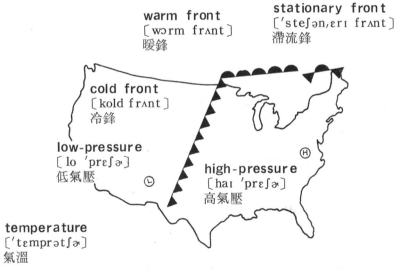

cold front
〔kold frʌnt〕
冷鋒

low-pressure
〔lo ˊprɛʃɚ〕
低氣壓

high-pressure
〔haɪ ˊprɛʃɚ〕
高氣壓

temperature
〔ˊtɛmprətʃɚ〕
氣溫

Fahrenheit
〔ˊfærənˌhaɪt〕
華氏

centigrade／Celsius
〔ˊsɛntəˌgred〕／〔ˊsɛlsɪəs〕
攝氏

atmospheric pressure
〔ˌætməsˊfɛrɪk ˊprɛʃɚ〕
氣壓

⑱四季 *Four Seasons*

summer
〔'sʌmɚ〕
夏

spring
〔sprɪŋ〕
春

fall
〔fɔl〕
autumn（英）
〔'ɔtəm〕
秋

winter
〔'wɪntɚ〕
冬

INDEX

D

E

H

I

J

K